THE BONE BOX

BY
ITAMAR BERNSTEIN

BookSurge Publishing

THE BONE BOX

BookSurge Publishing (October 2006.)

ISBN-10: 1419649221
ISBN-13: 978-1419649226

For my wife Judy

THE BONE BOX

1

If I hadn't been on duty that autumn Saturday evening at the district police headquarters on the Russian compound in Jerusalem, I would probably never have known what an ossuary was, the momentous importance that one such archeological artifact could assume, and the turmoil it would create in my life.

It was already dark in the city and the Sabbath was out when I was sent to investigate a burglary at the Rockefeller archeological museum. The building was located in Sultan Suleman street, by the North Eastern corner of the Old City wall, near the Flower Gate. I boarded my clunker at the parking lot of the police district headquarters, and it took me ten minutes to drive to the museum through the dark, deserted and oppressive streets of East Jerusalem.

The museum was already closed for visitors when I entered the rectangular inner courtyard, which was flanked on both sides by arched entranceways. A middle aged man came out of an entrance facing me.

"Police, I presume?" he said.

"Affirmative. Inspector Inbar, Michael Inbar," I ventured.

"Pretty somber, aren't you Inspector? I'm Zalman Ganot, Israel Antiquities Authority. We have the responsibility for the storerooms, archive and library here. This is just a small burglary. Follow me if you don't mind, and I'll show you."

He turned around and reentered the building through the same arched entrance that he came from. I followed him into a round room with a domed ceiling and cornices adorned with white tiles, bearing an inscription all around, which looked Greek. Noticing my weary look at this, Zalman expounded

"A quote from Plato. First known occurrence of the Greek word 'archeology'."

"Uh," I muttered. It was still Greek to me. "Did they break any entrance door to the museum that you know, Mr. Ganot?"

"Nah. The museum was open today from 10 a.m. to 2 p.m. You're free to inspect the doors, Inspector" he proposed somewhat sarcastically. "But I believe they just went down to the storeroom and broke open the gate. This way."

Now he led me through some exhibition halls with high windows resembling a cathedral. Then we went to another hall, which I thought must have been the library, featuring arched supporting columns that looked like medieval structures from crusaders' period I've seen around the country. I noticed the cork floors everywhere, undoubtedly intended to reduce noise.

"Are we getting down to the heart of the matter? I'm tired, Ganot."

"You seem to be a perpetually lethargic person, Inspector. What's the matter with you, enjoy this visit in a great museum. You're getting it for free. Here we go."

He descended a flight of stairs, and stopped before an iron gate in the basement.

"It's all yours" said Zalman. "Do your stuff."

It was an iron sliding grille constructed to block the entire height and width of the corridor type entrance to the basement. Upon close inspection I could clearly see that the lock was broken. I dusted it carefully for possible fingerprints and asked Zalman what, if anything, was stolen. He said it was a burial box, called an ossuary. As we went inside the storeroom he explained to me that an ossuary is a small chest, usually of wood or stone, and usually 50 to 80 centimeters in length, 28 to 50 centimeters in height, made just to contain the bones of a human burial. Such ossuaries were used for a secondary disposition of the bones. Bodies were usually placed first on a ledge in a burial cave. The dry bones that remained were collected about a year after the first burial and put in an ossuary for a second, permanent burial. The ossuary was invariably placed in a burial cave, not the same burial cave where the body was first laid. This practice of secondary burial was the rule among Jews in Palestine mostly between 20-15 B.C. to about 70 A.D., and possibly to 135 A.D. for those in Jerusalem. Elsewhere this custom probably continued until the third and fourth century. The reason for the double burial was apparently that most Jews, especially in the first century, believed in resurrection of the dead, which meant literally that the bones of the dead bodies shall rise. Given such conceptions it is understandable that the gathering and keeping of the bones in an ossuary would seem appropriate.

We were indeed in the most appropriate place for a lecture on this subject, since the huge storeroom was stocked with endless rows of ossuaries placed on wooden shelves.

Zalman showed me a small empty space on a wooden shelf.

"Here lay the ossuary which the burglars took," he indicated. "This one bore the name 'Matya' in Hebrew script. "

"I guess Matya is a contraction of the name Matityahu. Zalman. Anyone important, that you know?" I queried.

I deduced from the evidence I noticed by the empty shelf that the burglars were probably disturbed mid work, as they seemed to have left in some hurry. But I wasn't going to share this elementary perception with Zalman here. This was getting tiresome, and I felt like returning home and hitting bed to try to fall asleep. I wasn't surprised when Zalman answered that the name Matya was one of the most common names found on Jewish ossuaries in Palestine, and that the ossuary stolen was probably of no great value. I turned to go home, then had the presence of mind to ask Zalman where this particular ossuary was originally found. He indicated a certain address in the suburb of East Talpiot. I said they should have posted a guard around if they care for these bone boxes to stay put, took my leave of Zalman and returned to the parking lot of the museum to board my clunker and drive to my apartment in Tel Arza, a few minutes away past the orthodox quarter of Mea

Shearim, where I saw many Hasidic Jews walking the streets after the Sabbath conclusion service of Arvit.

I entered my apartment wearily and went to sleep. But after I slept about three hours the phone began buzzing. The time was 9:25 PM, so, with some hesitation, I picked it up on the third ring. My recently separated wife, Leora, was on the line. She instructed me , tersely but intensely, to turn my TV on , and hung up. I figured that she was acting overdramatic, obeyed mechanically as usual and punched "power" on my TV remote control. The morbid face of the TV news anchorman filled the screen as he announced sternly that prime minister Rabin had just been assassinated at a peace rally in Tel Aviv. I blurted "Oh God, and Guy would have been twenty two tomorrow," punched the TV off and escaped to my bed.

I tossed and turned in bed, but couldn't fall asleep, as every night since my personal tragedy happened in mid summer of that same year.

My son had been suffering from a severe depression for several months, and I did sometime fear the worst. So when my wife called me at work on that evening and said that his room was locked and he wouldn't respond to calling his name and knocking on the door, death immediately reared in my mind and my heart palpitated with a pang. I shouted my son is dead and started sobbing savagely and uncontrollably. My secretary hurriedly drove me home. Someone climbed to the rear window of his room and broke it, then immediately screamed to call the paramedics. Leora ran to Guy's room, the secretary following on the steps.

Leora came out of the room crying hysterically, her pain throbbing around me. The paramedics came and she reentered the room with them, but they could only confirm Guy's death. I howled even more but did not have the strength of mind to even think about entering Guy's room. I ran up and down, back and forth in the house. Sat, stood up, sat again, lay down on the floor and twisted in all forms and directions. But I could not escape the terrible situation. I screamed for my son and hoped that he would immediately come out of the room. I saw Leora breaking out from Guy's room dashing past everyone in the corridor ripping her hair and rushing to our bedroom, door slamming behind her. And I still twisted around in frenzy.

This is not true, how do I get out of this nightmare, my mind raged. Where do I hide now for eternity?

At nights I could not sleep, daydreaming deliriously about my son in conversation and activity with me. During the day I had to face all those annoying friends and colleagues who honestly, with good intentions, were torturing me with the meaningless words all of them repeated endlessly as if they had rehearsed together.

"You have your family to take care of, as well as your police work. Be strong."

As if I needed to be told all this. Were it not for these cursed obligations I would emulate Guy's suicide and be immediately released from the pain. And anyway how could I betray his memory by tending to things as meaningless and trivial as personal achievement, status and career?

The constant, unbearable, relentless pain weighing down on my chest like a hundred tanks parked on it. And the need to perform work and other daily duties, was now utterly meaningless: to watch people going places, coming back, talking and toiling for reasons that now completely escaped me.

What is the meaning of all this hassle and tussle? I am dead and these people continue their daily occupations and I have to watch them in their utterly stupid ambitions and activities. To get rich, to be powerful, to do this and that. What for, as life has already ended? And why is it that I'm dead and they're alive? Why is it they have sons to continue their existence after they're gone, and where is mine?

While performing my duties as a police inspector, I would feel sad, enraged, empty headed and exalted, concurrently or alternatively.

Why cannot I also depart after Guy, maybe I will find him somewhere. But, when I call him back in my dreams, he only signals that it was time for him to go on with his passage, and not me. I have family, duties, and a city's population to protect here. The same population who couldn't honestly give a damn about Guy's death. Can anyone understand this city's treatment of me?

As the weeks and months passed, black horror settled in my mind. My own darkness engulfed, sucked and suffocated me. Inescapable misery constantly bashing my heart, gashing wounds of unbearable pain. Memories of my son melted my brain like butter in boiling vapor, driving me insane. And the worst was the impossibility, the absolute impossibility to run away, vanish, disappear. There was nowhere to hide, except if blessed sleep came to me some nights after many hours of twisting in my bed. No appetite, for food, sex or achievement, whatsoever. No ambition to make even the slightest advance. Only the burden in my chest getting heavier every day and the nagging dread that in time I will forget Guy and desert him.

And so I continued living a zombie, grieving not only the loss of my son, but mainly the loss of my old securities, of the confident man I used to think I was. Of how I imagined I could make life happen. Slowly I began realizing that I was separated from life because my son was my life and he would never return. I had lost my connection to the part of myself that I could not, without my son, satisfy and mourned that part of myself which my son had reflected. I mourned for myself. This was the unfolding of the simple realization of why I felt dead among the living.

I went to the kitchen, took a sleeping pill, sagged back inside my bedroom and sank into a welcome dreamless sleep.

2

On the next day I joined my buddy Jonathan Dayan for lunch at Taami restaurant. It was a real institution in Jerusalem, serving quick lunches for about thirty years under the management of the same family from the same unassuming location on Shamai street. Jonathan had to drive over from his office at the national police headquarters on Mount Scopus, while I just walked over from my office in the Russian compound. The service at Taami was always rushed, but very efficient, which suited us just fine for lunch breaks. We went back a long time, to our service together as pilots with the air force. We joined the police about the same time, but Jonathan now made it to the relatively major position of a chief inspector, rubbing with the highest echelons of the country's police and with the Minister of Interior. At the sight of my haggard appearance he inquired what I was doing these days.

"Nothing much, Jonathan. I have to investigate a routine burglary that took place yesterday at the Rockefeller museum. "

"And you would have preferred to investigate, say, the Rabin assassination?"

"Not really. From what I hear, it's an open and shut case. That zealot nuthead killed the prime minister, slam dunk. Of course in 10 years someone will surface with some wild conspiracy theory, as they always do in this type of case, worldwide. The assassin could not have acted alone, blah blah. Anyway, everyone and everything was born to die, so what's the big commotion. Best to die as soon as possible and save the totally unnecessary pain of living."

"Let it go, Michael. You're not responsible for Guy's death, any more than I'm responsible for Rabin's assassination."

Flashback of Guy indirectly telling me that the Prozac I suggested he should   take was causing him an urge to commit suicide. His psychiatrist came to us hours after Guy died and covertly removed the Prozac pills from his room. Then about two weeks after the suicide, at his office, that same psychiatrist was evoking the possibility that we sue him and the Prozac manufacturer for wrongful death. I subsequently learned that many experts believe some people act upon an irresistible urge to commit suicide after taking Prozac for several weeks. I felt cold sweat on my scalp, but said nothing on this subject. My guilt feelings were justified, and I deserved to be tortured by them for the rest of my life. I turned the   conversation around.

"Aren't you responsible, Jonathan? If anything is an open question on that one, it's the obvious failure of the security service to effectively protect Rabin. But that's indeed not a   direct responsibility of the police. The venerable Shin Beth screwed up. Ha Ha."

"All I'm suggesting is maybe if you took some more responsibility at work, that would help to alleviate your pain over Guy's death."

"Dying and decaying would be the only way to remove the constant unbearable burden from my chest. My mind and body are rotting. Everyone around me, including you, knows that of course. But nobody would dare to acknowledge it."

At that point Jonathan was waiving his hand to a young woman who entered the little restaurant. She swayed her ripe hips in a somewhat awkward, slanted gait over to us. Jonathan invited her to join our table. She stared directly into my eyes. What look! She offered her hand to me, proclaiming

"Rona Argov, homicide."

"Michael Inbar, zombie. But in my prior life I would probably be tempted."

"I'm used to smart guys word playing with my last name, which of course, with some male chauvinist imagination, means 'love-maker' in Hebrew. I've heard a lot about you, inspector. Not very tall, are you?"

"I wonder how you noticed that when I'm seated," I actually laughed. "Sit down already and you'll make me feel much more suitable. "

She complied. We all ate the Hummus, a pedigree in Jerusalem. Sublime Hummus that we took with a layer of warm chickpeas on top, accompanied by fresh pita, pickles and onions. The high point of my day was consuming this best Hummus in town in that company, and the low point was that I did have to return to work after that.

It was almost midnight two days later when the phone ringing woke me up. It was chief inspector Dayan. He said there was another burglary at the Rockefeller museum. But this time it was a very serious matter, because the newly hired guard at the museum was murdered during the robbery. Dayan said he wants me to investigate the case. I protested that I wasn't really into it, that it's been a while since I left homicide department for the easier stuff, that I'm rusty, whatever. But he insisted I should and could do it. Finally I tired of the argument and agreed to go and have a look.

When I came to the museum there were already a couple of guys from homicide there. The body of the guard lay strewn on the cork floor at the library. The sliding grille gate to the storeroom was broken again. My acquaintance Zalman showed me the empty space on the shelf. This time it looked like several ossuaries were missing. But when I asked Zalman for details, he said we should discuss this back at the museum's meeting room. The room with the Greek inscription of Plato. So we went back to that room at the southwest corner of the museum. He closed the doors, sat down on one of the chairs at the small round table in the middle of the room, under the domed ceiling, and invited me to sit down on the opposite chair,

"This is difficult for me, Inspector Inbar. Personally I really want you to succeed in this investigation. But I'm under strict instructions to give you only limited information on this matter."

"And why is that? How many ossuaries were stolen tonight?"

"Eight."

"Were they also inscribed with names?"

"Five of them were inscribed with legible names."

"What about the other three?"

"Can't elaborate on that"

"What names were there on the five ossuaries that you acknowledge were inscribed?"

"Can't tell you that."

"Did these ossuaries have anything in common?"

"Next question, please."

"Where did each of the ossuaries come from?"

"Can't talk about their provenance, either. But I can assure you they're authentic."

"What do you mean by that, Zalman?"

"Many artifacts in this country have been found to be fake. We deem them suspect especially when their provenance is unknown. That is not the case regarding the ossuaries stolen tonight. They are all kosher."

"Do you have the bones that were placed in these ossuaries, respectively?"

"The official position of the Antiquities Authority will be that there was no substantial finding of bones in these ossuaries."

"What does that mean? I thought you told me ossuaries were made precisely to retain the bones. Don't you usually find bones in these ossuaries? "

"We do. But in deference to religious precepts, they are usually given Jewish burial as soon as possible, Inspector Inbar. I believe the law in Israel prescribes that skeletal remains found in ossuaries be reburied. Sometimes, in special findings, they're not."

"Was this the case with the subject bones?"

"Can't discuss this point any further."

" Big help you are, Zalman. I guess I'll take off. I wanted to pass on this case, but this incredible refusal to cooperate with me is truly inciting. Incidentally, were there any other artifacts originally found with any of these ossuaries?"

"Specify, please?"

"Don't play dumb on me, Zammy. I mean, like pottery shards, lamps, coins, et cetera. You know. The things they always exhibit in archeological museums?"

"I'll take the fifth on this one, too. Oh, sorry, I came originally from the U.S. That means I have a right to remain silent, and on this point I'll use it, too. If you have no further questions, we can both go home now, Inbar. I assure you again that there was nothing personal in my limited cooperation with you tonight. If ever you need my help in this investigation, don't hesitate to ask. Unless specifically instructed to take the fifth again, I'll be happy to provide you as much information as I can. " He gave me his business card.

"Keep your pants on, Zalman." I ejaculated bitterly. "Macho man."

I went home and slept on it. On the next morning I called Chief Inspector Dayan and told him I'll take charge of the investigation until I delve to the very bare bones of this strange matter.

3

And so it happened that on the   fifth day after Rabin's assassination , around noon, I left my apartment in central Jerusalem and drove directly to East Talpiot. It was located five kilometers south of my place, about half way between Jerusalem and Bethlehem. I parked my car at Yad Harutzim street, in the industrial zone, and walked over to the eastern part of the town, an area popularly called Governor's Mansion. Walking a distance always makes it easier to detect unwanted shadows. By the time I got to the address Zalman gave me for the provenance of the Matya ossuary, on Dov Gruner street, I was sure nobody was following me.

It was a four story apartment building that looked neither new nor   old. I rang the bell of a ground floor apartment and a   young woman opened the door. I heard a baby crying inside the apartment.

"Sorry to bother you," I made out. "I'm inspector Inbar, from Jerusalem's police. I'm investigating some matter having to do with the location of this building. Nothing to do with you personally, but maybe you can provide me with some information."

She showed me inside the apartment and we sat down on couches in the living room, facing each other across a small coffee table. The baby heard our small talk and stopped crying. I accepted her offer for coffee and she walked over to her kitchen to make it.

"And what precisely are you looking for, Inspector Inbar?" she asked while filling the kettle with water, her back turned to me.

"Something to do with a cave apparently located right below this very apartment building."

She turned around, facing me. "I never heard of such cave. But I know that some ancient burial caves were indeed found in this area. The most famous of those is the burial cave where six bone boxes were found in 1990, all bearing names of a notorious ancient priestly family, named Caiapha. One of those, belonging to a real High Priest, is prominently displayed at the Israel museum. It bears the name Joseph bar Caiapha."

"Never heard of him. I'll look for it on my next visit to that museum. Do you know when your apartment building was constructed?"

"1980. But I only came to live here after my marriage in 1987. People seem to move in and out of this neighborhood more frequently than in Jerusalem. Some don't really appreciate the close proximity to Bethlehem, I guess. In fact, we just contracted to sell this apartment a few weeks ago. "

"Is there any resident of this building you know of who purchased a new apartment back in 1980?"

"I'm afraid only Moshe Cohen . He's a sixty something widower living in apartment ten, third floor." She motioned to the ceiling.

"Thanks, then. I'll go and talk to him." I took her phone number, finished the coffee, and climbed the stairs to the third floor.

But when I rang the doorbell, it wasn't an aging man who opened. It was detective Rona Argov.

4

" What do you know, if that isn't our inspector again. Cherchez la femme?" She did look surprised, though she was trying to act casual.

"Hey, I'm surprised myself, Rona. I'm here on business. Police business. You?"

"I happen to be working on a case. Some guy who was found dead at a hotel in Cyprus yesterday. He happened to live in this very apartment before his demise, not really tragically early in his life."

"Gee. And when I saw you at the door my first thought was that you were pursuing a preference for older men."

"A gut reaction worthy of your apparent role model, Inspector Clouseau. Come inside already, will you."

I followed her slender and a bit taller than average figure into the living room. The room was basically standard. The usual couch and coffee table with a color brochure on it, one painting on the wall, a small bookshelf with some books and a lonely photo album.

"I'm sure you have the necessary search warrant, girl. Did you make good use of it?"

"Nothing thus far. Feel free to snoop around yourself."

I read the titles of the books on the shelf. Some novels, the usual Hebrew Bible. Picked up the photo album and viewed its contents. An old style album, like the one I had in my childhood, where I used to glue the photos on by their four edges. Nothing resembling Cyprus in it. But I noticed some pictures on a particular page were missing, apparently removed from their spaces. The wall painting seemed to represent old Jerusalem in its pre modern form, with a few Arabs leading two camels below the Tower of David. The brochure on the table featured a similar picture on the front cover, and bore the title <u>The Archeology of the New Testament</u>. It was dated 1978 for the edition, so it couldn't possibly refer to the specific ossuaries I was looking for.

I walked over the   apartment's small bedroom and searched it. There was a calendar book by the phone on the night table next to the bed. I opened it at the beginning of the previous month, and turned the pages forward. Not many events in the life of Moshe Cohen, evidently. Only the calendar page for October 14th of the same year. by the space for 10:00 AM, bore a scribbled line "last offer 272,000 dollars. " I tore it out and put it in my pocket , returned to the living room, sat on the sofa and straightened my regard at Rona, already sitting on the same sofa.

"Which hotel was the body found at, Rona?"

"Some place in central Nicosia, Cleopatra , if my recollection is correct. I asked for permission to go there next week. Takes some time with the office red tape, you know. Buying the tickets and paying my expenses and all that crap."

"Hey, I fly around on   most Saturdays, just to keep in form. I rent a   small plane at Herzlia airport, near Tel Aviv. Why don't I rent a somewhat more substantial machine this coming Saturday, and we can go together to Nicosia, find out what the late Mr. Cohen was up to."

"I think I prefer the experience of a commercial pilot over a weekend flyboy. But you're welcome to join me next week. At your private expense, of course. You know the police accountant is definitely not going to approve two love birds going on one plane."

I laughed and for some reason felt like telling her a joke.

"A- propos birds in planes, did you hear this one? A parrot and a man are seated next to each other in the first class of a jumbo crossing the Atlantic. The stewardess comes in and asks if anybody wants a drink. 'Bring me a cup of coffee, please,' the man requests. 'You ugly bitch, turn your fat ass around and bring me some Scotch. On the double, monkey face. And make it on the rocks,' squeaks the parrot. The overwhelmed stewardess hurries to the galley and brings a glass of whiskey for the parrot. 'I'm afraid you forgot my coffee,' ventures the man. 'Oh, sorry, be right back,' apologizes the stewardess. She turns to the galley but the parrot shouts after her, 'Bring me another glass of Scotch, whore' which causes her to again forget the coffee and bring only the whiskey. The man realizes that service on that plane is reserved to the rude, so this time he raises his voice a tad, and says, 'I second the impressions expressed by our friend the parrot here as to your appearance. You're anything but a movie star. Bring me that coffee at long last.' The stewardess decides she had enough abuse for one flight. She goes to the back of the plane, turns two levers, the seats of the man and the parrot revolve and expel them out of the plane. In the cold air, with the wind howling all around, the parrot screams at the man, 'For someone who can't fly, you sure are very impolite'."

Rona smiled at me for the first time and said "Okay., you managed to establish the disadvantage of a commercial flight in some ornithological situations. I will join you in flight to Nicosia on Saturday, and I hope I'll live to regret this decision. See you at that Herzlia airport, 7 A.M. sharp. Make sure that this airplane be a lot newer than your car."

5

I was greeted by a constant caroling of robins claiming possession of an oak tree in the middle of blooming fields on the beautiful Saturday morning when I parked my car at a spot inside the airport area in the little town of Herzlia, about nine kilometers north of Tel Aviv. It was a municipal airport, serving mostly local flights, situated somewhat east of the plush community of Kfar Shmaryahu, across the railroad to Haifa. I went over to the office of a company from where I used to rent planes on many such Saturdays, and rented a neat little Piper Cherokee Arrow. It had a range of 1600 kilometers and could easily make the flight to Nicosia, Cyprus. But I didn't tell them I was flying there, only that I'd return the plane in three days. Nor did I file a flight plan.

By the time I came out of the office Rona was standing there, the gentle sea breeze waving her long dark tresses. A drowsy sparrow chirped a halfhearted call note. I performed the walk around the plane, checking out the left wing, ailerons, left fuselage , tail, rudder, right fuselage, right wing, ailerons, gas tank, tires and propeller. Everything in order, tank full. I climbed to the left seat over the wing, and Rona did the same on the right side of the plane. Good girl. Called out "clear" and started the engine, taxied the plane to runway 11, stopped short of it, revved the engine and performed the final check. Proceeded to the runway and pushed the throttle all the way in. The engine responded eagerly and the plane accelerated on the tarmac. At 70 mph airspeed I pulled the stick up, held the left rudder in just a tad with my foot, and off we went into the clear sky. Turned the stick to the right while climbing, and we passed over the popular beaches of Herzlia, not very crowded in this time of year. Tel Aviv rolled out to our left as we were climbing at 875 feet per minute. When we got to 6000 feet I reduced rpm and lowered the stick a bit to level the plane, steadied speed at 230 kilometers per hour and took the VOR direction to Nicosia. I knew it was Visual Flight Rules all the way, wind calm, so it was going to be a real easy passage. Free as an eagle in the sky.

"What a great feeling to fly," exclaimed Rona, her black eyes blazing at me.

"Business before pleasure. Hope you didn't tell anybody we're going to Nicosia today. We'll just try to find whatever we can privately, incognito so to speak. And if it looks promising you can still go there again on an official visit to the local police."

"Will do. Coffee, Captain Clouseau?"

She opened her bag and brought out a thermos, poured hot coffee in two cups, held one and gave me the other.

"Great, my girl. Any other goodies you have in that bag?"

"Sure. I noticed at the table in Taami that your bite is bigger than your size." She took a sip from her cup. "The price tag for this little escapade must be steep, so I thought I'd contribute a little on that score."

My wife retained a big shot attorney soon after Guy's death, and this fellow got us a huge settlement from the Prozac manufacturer. The settlement agreement stipulated confidentiality, and I wasn't going to talk about it anyway. So I articulated,

"Show me the money, baby, or keep your hypothesis theoretical."

She took out a ham and cheese sandwich and brought it to my mouth.

"Now how on earth could you get ham in holy Jerusalem, baby?"

We both broke out laughing.

"That's for me to know and for you to find out," she said ,focusing that look straight into my eyes, where she held it all the way to Cyprus.

6

Several hours later I landed the Piper smoothly at a small airport near Nicosia. We took a taxi and Rona instructed the driver to drop us off at the Cleopatra hotel on Florinis street. He asked are we sure we want to go to that hotel, it's not a vacation hotel but rather for business travelers, as it is located near the business center of town. Rona told him we still want to go there because it is also closer to shops. Then he remained quiet until we came in front of the hotel. It was an unassuming five story building. We entered the lobby, registered as tourists from New York. Rona made for her best American accent and asked for room number 57. The clerk remarked that the room had two separate twin beds, Rona said fine. He gave us two keys, indicating the way to the elevators. We waited for an elevator a minute with some other people, punched 5 when it came, exited to a rather long, empty and quiet corridor, unlocked and opened the door of room 57, and stepped in. So far so good.

It was a standard room with two twin beds and a bathroom, with a balcony facing the city. The room was neat and clean. We immediately began searching it, but although we did that very thoroughly and took our time, we could find nothing of interest in the room. Obviously the local police had already taken away whatever there was. We then went to the bathroom and searched it, with the same result.

By that time I felt my usual lethargy creeping on me. I went to the window, rolled the wooden shade down, emptied my bladder in the bathroom and went to sleep on the twin bed nearer the window. The sun was setting and some light still filtered through the shades, striping a broken shadow on the opposite wall, but that didn't bother me. I needed to relieve the feeling of a sword stuck deep in my heart, which was always in there, though the feminine presence with me today did seem to provide some relief that was gone now.

I must have slept a couple hours when Rona woke me up gently. She was smiling with youthful gaiety. Undoubtedly made some nice shopping while I was in dreamland.

"You can resume your dozing later, Michael. I used the toilet just now, but couldn't flush it. I lifted the lid and saw a paper stuck in the device that's supposed to allow refilling with water. It 's a picture of Mr. Cohen in a somewhat unusual setting. He must have hidden it in the toilet just before he was murdered. I guess we're no better than the Nicosia police, just luckier."

I rubbed my eyes, turned the reading light on, and peered at the paper she was holding. In it I recognized the face of Moshe Cohen, as I saw him in the album at his East Talpiot apartment. He was standing before the entrance of a cave, flanked by construction material and cranes.

"Bingo," I said to Rona. "Let's go celebrate that at a good restaurant in town. Take the picture with you."

7

The streets were humming with busy evening traffic when we took a taxi to the Taverna Eirinias, in the Strovolos area of Nicosia. There was only one course on the menu there, the Meza. We chose some of the approximately 25 dishes on offer, and washed these down with a bottle of local Ouzu. The restaurant was full with patrons, all doing the same, and nobody paid any attention to us. We both knew that the picture we found evidenced the connection between this murder in Nicosia and the burglary-murder at the Rockefeller museum. So now there was sound professional justification for our teaming together. And that was pretty cool, as far as I was concerned. Judging by the way Rona was again piercing me with her direct gaze into my eyes, she wasn't displeased with this fact, either.

By the time we took the taxi back to the hotel we were hugging in the back seat, and I was surprised after many months of total indifference to womanhood to find myself aroused by the thought that I may after all top this trip getting laid by this young woman.

Indeed we couldn't stop kissing even before we got to our room, and she seemed pretty impatient for me to stop fumbling for the key and open the door. When we finally entered the room and she eagerly lay on the bed nearer to the door, on her back, and her body language all but invited me to enter her, I was about to do so. But then she started crying. I rolled off and from her, stroked her hair and said I'm sorry. But she only continued crying. So I moved over in silence to my bed. As always, I found it very hard to fall asleep, but for once this wasn't the result of the sorrow and burden in my chest.

In the morning we left the hotel and took a taxi back to the airport. When Rona opened her handbag to pay the driver, the picture fell on the mat on its face. I picked it up and noticed a large mark drawn on it. It was shaped somewhat like the letter x, only tilted more sideways and with the lateral arm longer than the other.

It actually looked even more similar to the second letter in the Greek script next to the name of the town Achna in English listed as one of the destinations offered to prospective passengers on the side panel of the taxi. I handed the picture back to Rona and she replaced it in her handbag. She was all soft and feminine now. When we took off en route to Israel, at several thousand feet, she kissed my cheek and explained,

"The pen mark across the back of that picture is an exact drawing of the letter Taw, the last in the alphabet, in Paleo Hebrew script, which in simpler terms is ancient Hebrew writing. I hope that can make you happy today, darling, for whatever that knowledge is worth."

Beats me, I thought, But I surely liked her new tone.

8

The ride was much rougher on the return leg to Herzlia, with considerable turbulence, although I could still fly on Visual Flight Rules. But Rona kept her calm, and while I was turning base for landing said she would go back to Nicosia during the week to pay an official visit this time at the local police department. After we landed safely and I taxied the plane back to its assigned parking spot, she took Cohen's picture out of her handbag and put it in my shirt's pocket, kissed me on the right cheek and split, saying she's going to visit a friend in Tel Aviv. I went to the rental office , paid the bill in cash and returned to my apartment in Jerusalem. I powered my computer, scanned the back side of Cohen's photo, took out Zalman Ganot's business card and entered his email address, typed "Is this a symbol of some kind, Zalman?" in the message area, attached the scanned backside of the photo, clicked on "send" and went to bed, leaving the computer on.

Two evenings later Rona called me and informed that a day before he was murdered Moshe Cohen had a meeting with some jet set businessman called Seth Frankenheim. She sends me kisses and will return on the next morning's commercial flight to Ben Gurion airport.

I went to my computer, checked my email, opened and read a terse response from Ganot

"1 Samuel 21:14; Job 31:35; Ezekiel 9:4-6. Talmud, Shabbath 55a."

Hate playing riddles, my brain fulminated. Still I opened my Bible at the first passage, when David was much afraid of Achish the King of Gath, he feigned madness and "made marks (Taw in Hebrew) on the doors of the gate." I moved to the second passage, where Job says " Here is my signature," literally in Hebrew "Here is my Taw (mark)." I opened at the third passage, and found that in Ezekiel 9:4 the man clothed in linen is instructed to go through the city of Jerusalem and put a mark (Taw) upon the foreheads of the men who sigh and groan over the abominations committed in the city. In 9:5-6 the destroyers are told to touch no one upon whom is the mark (Taw.) The Talmud passage in reference tells of two Taws, and distinguishes between them as "a Taw of ink upon the foreheads of the righteous," and "a Taw of blood upon the foreheads of the wicked." In the same context a Rabbi is quoted in the explanation of the Talmudic passage "Taw stands for thou shalt live, Taw stands for thou shalt die."

I sighed and groaned myself probably more than these ancient characters did, over Zalman's abominations, and went to sleep mentally cursing him.

9

The rain was torrential on the next morning as I drove to Talpiot against the wind. Whirlwinds of water surrounded me and dripped under my chin as I parked my car at Oley Hagardom street and ran several blocks to the building on Dov Gruner street, in the same area of East Talpiot where it all began. I knocked on several ground floor doors, to no avail. I felt cold and wet and was about to return to the car and drive back to the comforting relative warmth of my office in Jerusalem, when the mailman came by. He was standing outside by the mailboxes, so I had to do the same , approaching him.

"Where is everybody today?" I asked. He responded with a smile, but did not open his mouth at all to address my concern. I realized that I should better raise my voice if I want him to hear me in the swelling gusts of wind and the loud blast of falling hail. So I repeated the same question, this time practically shouting into his ear.

"This apartment house has become my worst address, sir," he shouted back. "Seems everyone is moving out these days and I have a very hard time keeping track of them."

Lightning suddenly struck me, but it didn't come from the stormy sky. I remembered the woman I first questioned in her apartment telling me she just contracted to sell it, and Moshe Cohen's note about a last offer of 272,000 dollars flashed in the shivering grey cells under my wet balding crown. Of course! These days only real estate prices in Israel are routinely stated in US dollars. Somebody was buying out all the residents, and I could bet the barley farm his name was Seth Frankenheim.

I returned to my clunker and drove it back to central Jerusalem. Maybe it wasn't really a sign from heaven, but I could swear the storm was noticeably subsiding. By the time I parked near the government land registry office the torrent had reduced to a drizzle.

This office, open and accessible to the public, allows anybody to check the ownership of property. Indeed the registry offers vital information regarding each plot and subplot. Usually a quick query will reveal all information registered there, including ownership of the land, its size, rights relating to it, and all pledges, mortgages, and so forth.

I gave the address of the building to the clerk. She asked for the plot number and grimaced when I told her I don't have it. She said go and get it and turned around. But I called after her and said I'm a police officer on official business, and she submitted and went to look for the transcript. Ten minutes later I had it in my hand.

It recorded that the owner of all apartments in the building, including Moshe Cohen's, was now a certain company called "BC Development, Ltd."

Back in my office, I instructed one of my deputies to find out all information about Seth Farnkenheim's business activities and about the ownership of BC Development, Ltd. Then I went down to the office cafeteria for lunch. While munching a sandwich there, my cell phone rang a happy tune. Rona was on the line, saying she's back at Ben Gurion airport, taking a taxi to her friend Yael's in Tel Aviv, and come meet me there at around 6 P.M., sweetheart. Yael may not yet be back from work, so if I'm not already back from shopping, you'll find the key under the mat. It's a small private home on an inner alley by Chen boulevard, just off city hall square. She gave me the address and I promised to be there.

I returned to my office where I found a full list of Seth Frankenheim's companies, all foreign, under a picture of the man boarding a Learjet, and a note stating that BC Developments, Ltd., was a company registered with the Israel Registrar of Companies, which was in turn a wholly owned subsidiary of a Lichtenstein corporation, registered in Vaduz.

I went to the library and read some legal stuff about land ownership in Israel. This confirmed what I already knew generally, that transactions of State-owned land involving foreign lessees require the approval of a government entity, the Israel Lands Administration. Since about 93% of the land in Israel is state owned, for historical reasons, and this land is most commonly leased for long term, rather than sold, chances are that this procedure would also be required for the subject apartment building in Talpiot.

I closed the law books, took my coat, left the office and drove down to Tel Aviv, the city that never stops

10

Traffic was heavy that afternoon on the main highway to Tel Aviv, sixty kilometers down by the Mediterranean sea, but I got there on time. I parked my car by the east side of the tree lined boulevard, a few meters south of the enclosed alley that Rona mentioned, and found this little old house standing low among taller and boring rectangular four story apartment buildings. I rang the bell. Nobody answered but the key was under the mat, as promised. I entered the house, went to the living room and took a nap on the couch.

Rona apparently came in while I was dozing. Because I woke up with her lips on mine. She stirred my passion up so fast that I grabbed her and we made love right there on the sofa. I hardly had time for hoping she wasn't comparing my hasty performance with any slower hand she probably knew before me, when the doorbell rang. I put on my pants and opened the door.

The petite woman by the door gave my naked torso an appreciating gaze and offered her hand , protesting,

"And Rona said she found you anything but sexy the first time she met you. Hi, I'm Yael. Nice to meet you, Michael. Consider me available when this femme fatale drops you, as she invariably does with her men."

Rona called loudly from behind "I'm taking a shower, and after that I'll go to dinner with my man. So you can eye him all you want until I freshen up, Yael."

When she came out ten minutes later I went into the same bathroom, after Yael handed me a fresh towel. By the time I exited with the towel around my waist, Rona called,

"Come in here and tell me which of the dresses I bought today you want me to wear for you tonight, my man."

I went in the bedroom where she was standing as God created the woman, but for a towel knotted over her wet long curls. I chose a red dress for her. She handed me a black shirt, a pair of French labeled leather pants, and short boots, commenting she'd like me looking dramatic. In other circumstances I would have felt like Zorro if I dressed up like that, but with this exciting woman along I felt looking appropriate and pretty elated.

Yael then drove us with her car to the best rated restaurant in Israel and when she dropped us off at the door, she commented,

"Take a taxi back, beautiful people. With all the wine I know you'll be drinking here, you're gonna need it."

The Casbah restaurant on Yirmiahu street served Moroccan-French food in a romantic setting, and we were both very much in the mood, sitting in a private booth, drinking much red wine and gazing into each other's eyes. The scene reminded me of "Casablanca," but the manager, probably sensing the electric chemistry between us that night, instead aired "Lady in Red," which I could have written myself there and then.

We couldn't stop kissing all the way in the backseat of the taxi, and when we came to the bedroom at Yael's, we made delirious love all through the rest of that night.

When I woke up late on the next morning, I called my secretary and asked her to arrange a meeting with the local director at the office of the Israel Lands Administration, responsible for processing transactions of real estate in Talpiot. She called back when I was drinking my morning coffee in Yael's kitchen, while Rona was soundly asleep. The secretary said she fixed me an appointment with a deputy director, named Bender, at 11:45 A.M. I took a gulp of coffee, shaved and dressed hastily, and took off to Jerusalem, without waking Rona. I got to the Administration's office a bit late, but Bender's secretary let me into his office. It was noonish, and he was sitting behind the center of the horizontal part of a T shaped conference desk, munching a sandwich. He motioned for me to sit at the outer tip of the vertical desk. I wondered if that was some sort of a phallic communication.

"What can I do you for, Inspector?" he pronounced.

I gave him the address and lot number of the building in Talpiot, where the late Moshe Cohen used to live.

"I need to know if your office has approved the purchase of this building by a company named BC Development, Ltd."

"It's under consideration," he answered after checking his computer. "It will probably be approved. What makes that transaction a police matter?"

"I have good reason to believe this company is behind a burglary-murder I'm investigating."

"I'll write that down as a factor for consideration, if you can provide this office with further information. Or, rather, if the office of the state Attorney General concretely endorses your apparently premature suspicion. Anything else?"

"Did this company file any special request regarding its future plans for this location?'

He took a moment to answer, then said "They stated they want to demolish the apartment building and build a small private museum instead. That would also require approval by the city zoning commission."

I decided I'd had it for the day and went to watch "Braveheart" in one of Jerusalem's movie theaters. Then I returned home, called Rona and asked her to meet me next on Saturday at the main entrance of the Israel Museum.

12

"Which part of the museum would you like to see first, Michael" asked Rona as we met on Saurday morning.

"The bone boxes."

"I believe the museum has some real ancient ones, from the Chalcolitic period, and others from the late Second Temple Period, before and during the first century."

I remembered that Zalman Ganot was talking about the latter, so I said,

"Second Temple Period."

We went to the part of the museum exhibiting the Roman period of occupation of the country, and I saw several limestone bone boxes, similar to the hundreds of boxes I saw inside the basement storeroom at the Rockefeller museum.

One especially ornamented box was inscribed in Hebrew characters on one side "Yehosef bar Caiapha," I remembered what the young woman at the Talpiot apartment told me about it, so I indicated it to Rona, articulating

"This box was found in a family tomb in East Talpiot. It contained the bones of a High Priest."

"Of course. Joseph bar Caiapha, the High Priest who was mostly involved with Jesus' trial by Pontius Pilate. The trial that led to his crucifixion by the Romans. He is mentioned not only by the historian Josephus Flavius as the longest serving High Priest in the first century, but also notoriously in the New Testament."

Like most Israelis I never read the New Testament, so this was something I didn't know.

"If you're done enjoying these relics of death, let's go see the Dead Sea Scrolls exhibition," insisted Rona.

She took me by the hand to the separate museum building called Shrine of the Book. It was a dome covering a structure that is two thirds below the ground, reflected in a pool of water surrounding it. We descended a flight of stairs, past a short corridor, into a round chamber just below the dome. The centerpiece of this exhibition was the Great Isaiah Scroll, which I knew was written by the Essene sect in Qumran on the shore of the Dead Sea, about a hundred years before Common Era. It contained the entire Old Testament book of Isaiah in legible Hebrew characters, which most Israelis could easily read. We approached this scroll, and Rona was actually perusing the written text. Then she touched my shoulder with her left hand, and with the right hand indicated a particular section of the scroll.

"Look Michael. Look at that!"

"What, that?"

"This. See the marks on the margin in here, and in here, and here?"

Then I saw it. A whole series of marks on the margins of different parts of the Great Isaiah Scroll manuscript. We counted eleven of them in columns XXVI, XXXV twice, XXXVIII, XLI, XLV, XLVI twice, XLVIII and LIII. They were all identical in shape to the X mark scribbled sideways with one longer arm on the back of Moshe Cohen's picture. His actual death warrant.

The mark of the Taw.

13

We were discussing the significance of the Taw mark over coffee at the museum restaurant. I explained,

"Listen Rona. From a passage of chapter nine in the book of Ezekiel I understand that the Taw mark designates those who are faithful to God, and it puts them under his protection for deliverance. The passage says it's a mark on the forehead."

"Maybe this mark had a similar connotation for the Essene scribes of the Dead Sea Scrolls, who according to the general consensus of experts were contemporaries of the Maccabees, second to first centuries before the common era, though some experts date them rather to the first century , common era" she offered pensively.

The older man sitting at the table next to us said,

"I apologize for interjecting in this interesting discussion. I couldn't avoid overhearing it. I agree that this understanding of the word "taw," a mark, in Ezekiel 9:4 as the last alphabetic character in ancient Hebrew script has a sound basis. I believe the markings on the Isaiah scroll you just saw are some form of symbolism based on that passage.

In an ancient papyrus found in Egypt, known as the Cairo Document, there is a significant reference to this passage in Ezekiel. This document first alludes to the Book of Zecharia, and then continues with an explicit quotation of Ezekiel 9:4 , as follows 'And 'they that give heed unto Him' are 'the poor of the flock'. These shall escape in the time of the visitation, but they that hesitate shall be given over to the sword when the Messiah of Aaron and Israel shall come. As it happened in the epoch of the visitation of the forefathers, which He said by the hand of Ezekiel: 'to set the mark upon the foreheads of such as sigh and groan'."

"I know this Damascus Document is a work that doubtlessly represents in general the same movement as that of the Qumran community, which authored the Dead Sea Scrolls," said Rona. " Is the time of visitation an eschatological term?" She lost me on this one.

"Yes. As other statements in the Damascus Document make plain, the time of visitation is the Last Judgment. When that time comes and the Messiah appears, the circumstances of the destruction of Jerusalem as described by Ezekiel will be repeated, which means that only those marked with the Taw on their foreheads will be saved. "

"That sounds to me like a purely figurative expression," opined Rona.

"Maybe. But at least one expert believes it is possible that the Taw mark was literally put upon the foreheads of the members of the Qumran community, as a sign to guarantee their salvation in the final judgment. I think that would have been done perhaps at the time of their final acceptance as full members of the community."

"So in your opinion, Taw for these Essenes was a mark standing for protection, deliverance and salvation. That's a really illuminating proposition. I, we, thank you very much indeed. "

"You're very welcome."

He stood up, reached to his pocket for some money, left it on his table and walked out of the cafeteria in energetic steps, lifting his hand in a farewell motion to us.

"Let's go to the Dead Sea now," proposed Rona happily. "I'd like to be alone with you on a remote beach. And that's the closest I can think of for a Saturday afternoon."

I mused that it would indeed be difficult to find a more remote place than the bleached wilderness below the steep limestone cliffs by the placid waters of the Dead Sea. It was barely an hour's drive away. I glanced at my watch. The time was 11:15 A.M.

"Why not. We'll get there for lunch in one of the hotels or in a little restaurant I know at the small shopping center in the hotels area. Then we'll hit whatever beach you like. Let's take my car."

"I don't mind riding in that ancient Italian machine, which you must have purchased from Leonardo da Vinci himself, as long as you do the driving, darling."

We walked back to take our respective cars in the museum's parking lot, drive them to her apartment, pack our bathing suits, leave her car and roll down to the sea by way of Jericho in mine. I was so exuberant in her company that I paid little attention to the burly man who was walking away from my clunker.

14

I was driving down the spectacular road eastward from Jerusalem to Jericho, intending to go from its start around 800 meters above sea level to its end at 300 odd meters below sea level, a distance of about 40 kilometers, in about 45 minutes. But we never got to Jericho that day.

From Jerusalem's Mount of Olives , the road winds downward toward Jerusalem's Shayyah neighborhood, where we came in view of the entire Judean hills wilderness, and the deep rift valley of the Jordan river.

Rona pushed the plastic power button of the old radio, and a singer's voice celebrated with us,

"On a clear day you can see forever."

The road was narrow, steep, rough and barren, winding below imposing limestone cliffs. I was still going to make it easily, as I did innumerable times. But while I was negotiating one particularly tight downward turn, I felt my foot go down to the floor on the brakes. The car was accelerating wildly, I shouted that I can't slow down and pulled the hand break out, but that didn't do much good. Rona clutched my right shoulder, but didn't utter a sound. We were zooming down in zigzags at an increasingly crazier speed. A large tourists' bus was coming up the hill toward us. I realized I can only avoid collision with it if I slow down fast. So I veered to the right, doing my best to decelerate the car as gradually as I could by making the widest possible contact of its right side doors against the sidewall.

But the bus was closing in and was now protruding into my lane making a wide turn just below us. I knew I must stop cold now, pulled harder on the steering toward Rona and heard a single shriek from her. The car flipped over to the left side of the road, narrowly missing the climbing bus, the roof hit against the vertical limestone and I passed out.

When I regained consciousness and crawled out of the car, my eyes dazzled with the blinding bright light reflected from the white cliffs around me and from the bleached valley and the Dead Sea below. My throat dried in the heat and the dust filmed in my ears, nostrils and mouth. But my heart was cold with fear for Rona, who was pulled out of the passenger seat and now lay motionless on the ground behind me. Like a wounded white dove.

15

"Are you awake, Michael?"

I opened my eyes and saw Jonathan Dayan sitting by my bed in what was clearly a hospital room. He was examining my face with concern. A smile curled his mouth when I answered,

"Sure enough. But I don't remember how the hell I got here. Where's Rona?"

"In the intensive care unit. Her husband is there with her, but she's still unconscious. The doctors say she has nothing broken. "

"I want to see her. What husband?"

"Her ex. She got divorced about six months ago. You can't see her now. The doctors say you should rest."

"I wanna see her." I tried to sit up in the bed, but he held my shoulders gently and forced me to lay my head back on the pillow.

"All in good time. Stay here for as long as they allow you, and then return home and take an even longer sick leave. By that time she'll hopefully be fine, and then you can go for a long vacation together. Ain't I the greatest matchmaker?"

"Get her doctor here, will you buddy?"

"Will do."

I turned my back on him and heard him stepping out of the room without closing the door.

I was having a nightmare, or was it a nightmare?

A stern faced doctor was telling me that brain tests were performed on Rona, because she's in a coma. The test results show her brain stem is damaged. She's in a vegetative state , can't breath and eat on her own so she's being held alive by machines, a ventilator and a breathing tube.

Oh God, I want to die now, my mind hollered. But before I die, I want to have revenge, not only against that burly man who obviously tampered with the braking mechanism of my car at the museum's parking lot yesterday, but against the whole world. I want to know that all life on this earth has ended. Let me feel the end of all times. I do not want to be the sole, extreme loser of God's extravagance. Suffer forever the unbearable misery of the unfathomable guilt for the deaths of my loved ones. Let me witness the reversal of this planet to its primal, chaotic darkness!

I continued living in this nightmare and died every moment of my existence in the darkness of oblivion, until a medical miracle happened several weeks later, and a nurse shouted in my ear that Rona awoke from her coma, and wanted to see me.

16

Before I entered Rona's room, the nurse told me doctors had weaned her off the ventilator in the past week. She can intake air, but she can't swallow on her own. The nurse said the doctors thought all the time that Rona was in an irreversible vegetative condition, and asked her ex husband whether he wants to remove her from life support. But the man, a lawyer, said he believes that medical science is not that certain, there was no rush. He said they should give her time. He wanted the doctors to take a step back, let the whole process slow down. Then, said the nurse, I first noticed a change in Rona's condition on Wednesday last. More medical tests were performed Thursday, and it appears her condition has dramatically improved. She has now recovered enough to communicate, which is rare in patients with such brain stem injuries. It is even more improbable that such patients will recover fully enough to feed themselves and live ordinary lives. The worst of it may be that she would never be able to walk. But Rona's just in the right place for miracles here in Jerusalem, isn't she?

I opened the door and walked in. Rona was asleep, her long black locks gracing the pillow. I turned around and took one step to the door, when I heard her softly calling my name. She was smiling faintly when I turned again to look at her, and said distinctively,

"Kiss me, my love."

Tears of joy filled my eyes. I walked over to her bed and kissed her on the lips.

"How are you, Michael."

"I'm fine."

"I want you to let your ghosts go, so that you will get your life back. You can't keep Guy alive forever, and you can't make me whole again."

"No my darling. I won't forsake Guy, the extension of my physical being, and I won't leave you, my soul mate."

I was sobbing violently.

"Go to your office tomorrow and continue our investigation."

"I don't know why we did it in the first place. Following these old bones led to this. What for?"

"For the truth. I want to find the truth. Isn't that what you wanted too?"

"If I continue this search now, it isn't going to be for the same reason."

"Our forefathers taught us we should be patient and considerate, even with those who aren't exactly friends. We should control our violent emotions, not the other way around."

"I'm no saint. Is there anything you want me to do for you now?"

"I'm still intrigued by the Taw marks on the Great Isaiah Scroll. I should have done more research as to their precise symbolism, in context."

"I'll find this out for you."

"Good. Now leave, because I'm really tired. Oh, take the keys to my car. You can use it as your antique has probably been taken to the Jericho museum. It's in my purse on the night table beside my bed here."

I took the keys out of her purse and exited her room, asked the nurse for access to a computer, and used it to send an email to Zalman Ganot, as follows:

"Hi Zalman. Michael again. What is the meaning of the eleven different Taw marks on the margins of the Great Isaiah Scroll?"

I left the hospital , took a taxi to the street where Rona lived. Spotted her fairly newer model Subaru parked there and drove it back to my apartment. Then I made a few phone calls, and found that my car was towed to a certain junkyard in Jericho

17

The next morning I took my Nikon and drove Rona's Subaru to the junkyard. A polite Arab indicated my Alfa to me, and I walked over to that relic with great apprehension about its mechanical condition. The roof was badly indented, but when I opened the hood I saw the engine was intact. With a sigh of relief I concentrated my regard on the master cylinder.

To increase safety, most modern car brake systems are split into two circuits, with two wheels on each circuit. If a fluid leak occurs in one circuit, only two of the wheels will lose their brakes and the car is able to stop when the driver presses the brake pedal. The master cylinder provides pressure to both circuits of the car. This device in newer model cars uses two pistons in the same cylinder in a way that makes the cylinder relatively failsafe. If we had taken Rona's Subaru down the dangerous road to Jericho that fateful Saturday, the combination valve would have warned us about a problem with the brake system, and would also have done some other things to make the car safer to drive. But macho me had to drive a 1969 Alfa Romeo, of course. And whoever sent that burly man to tamper with its master cylinder system could count on that. Although the Alfa's master cylinder has a somewhat unusual mounting mechanism, pointing toward the rear of the vehicle instead of facing forward, this guy must have been well prepared and known his way around the mechanism.

For I could see clearly that the feeder lines were taken out of the device that allows them to   bring brake fluid down to the master cylinder. Therefore the servo lines couldn't carry the brake fluid to the two servos in the engine compartment. Consequently, when I applied the pressure on the brake pedal down that treacherous, winding road, it could not engage the servo booster designed to engage the hydraulics to the brake calipers, allowing the car to stop.

With an even heavier heart than usual, I took several pictures evidencing the sabotage. Went back to the junkyard's office, paid the expenses of towing and storage and asked them to tow the car to the police evidence storage garage in Jerusalem. They said tomorrow but I insisted the car be towed today. They agreed to do that for a very steep price in about three hours. I said fine, where can I spend three hours in this place? They said everyone goes to see   Tel as-Sultan, a 10,000 years old excavated settlement, discovered in the 1950s. I mused bitterly that this would be a good place indeed for a zombie like me to slumber, and walked over to the place they showed me.

When I got there, there was a guide telling a bunch of tourists that the little hill was created by the different layers of civilizations that built and lived on the spot from many thousands of years ago. It contained the oldest retaining wall ever excavated, as well as the world's oldest stairway.

I sighed and was about to leave, when I noticed two overdressed middle aged men standing at the other side of the hill, facing me. I remembered the picture I saw on my desk of the taller man, so I went over to him, and said,

"Nice finding you here, Frankenheim. Planning a stairway to the gallows, undoubtedly."

He looked amused, and made speciously,

"Not at this time, Inspector Inbar. Planning rather a cable car that will link this Tel to Mount Temptation yonder."

"Who's tempted? The soul of that poor Moshe Cohen that you dispatched to heaven over in Nicosia, tempted to make you join next door, Seth?"

"Hell can wait, as they say. Mount Temptation is the place where Jesus of Nazareth is said to have withstood the first and third temptations of his forty days of solitude, per the New Testament. You should do some reading of that scripture, Mr. Inbar. In the meantime, Mount Temptation is an easy uphill hike, and the Bedouins at the base of the mountain offer glasses of mint tea to strengthen visitors for the walk. Pilgrims also make sure to stop at the 2,000 year old sycamore tree before which, according to legend, Jesus paused during his sojourn through Jericho."

"And you're going to make a lot of dough off that."

"Look around you, Inspector. This wilderness has always been known as a place of prophecy. Something about the limestone cliffs, the burning sun, the clear sky bleached with heat urges many otherwise ordinary people to start soothsaying. I'm a prophet of capitalism, but I will bring a lot of money to your country. Tourism is already your second largest industry. But Christian oriented tourism has infinitely more potential, and they spend with delirious abandon in hard foreign currency. If I can bring an additional one million such tourists a year here, for example, your country's coffers would swell for more than the entire US financial aid it gets that year. Get my drift? Think of that."

He took his companion by the shoulder and they both descended the hill and disappeared into the white limousine waiting below. I scratched my head for a moment, then returned to the Subaru and drove it home, flicked the computer on and read another cryptic message from Zalman Ganot, as follows:

"Isaiah 32:1ff; 42:1ff; 42:5ff; 42:19ff; 44:28; 49:5-7; 55:3-4; 56:1-2; 56:3ff; 58:13ff; 66:5ff"

I replied to this email in the following language:

"I'm afraid you suffer from a severe case of brain diarrhea, Zalman. As far as I can tell, you have many, many ideas. But they're always all shit. Thanks , anyway."

Jesus, my own brain will soon explode, I thought. But I still went over to Rona at the hospital, hoping this would make her happy. She was indeed curious when I handed her Zalman's code. She asked me to get her a Bible from the nurse, and when I returned asked me to open it on Isaiah in reading distance from her face and leaf through the pages, when she tells me. I did that while enjoying the expression of pleasure on her face. After about 20 minutes she told me to put the book down and informed,

"This is interesting Michael."

" Good. And I wrote to Zalman that he's probably suffering from brain diarrhea."

"I'm afraid it's rather you who sometimes exhibits signs of cerebral constipation. But listen, I figure most of these passages indicated specifically by the Taw marks on the Great Isaiah Scrolls have in one way or another to do with messianic expectations."

18

Identifying the man who had tampered with my Alfa from the police database of thugs at our lab was a piece of cake the next day. Turned out he was one Oleg Brukhin, living in the coastal town of Rishon Lezion, about 12 kilometers southeast of Tel Aviv.

It took me about 50 minutes to reach the outskirts of this town of a quarter million inhabitants, many of them Russian immigrants. A large sign by the roadside greeted visitors welcome, proclaiming that the name of the town originates from the book of Isaiah, 41:27. Definitely this prophet wasn't about to get out of my hair.

I parked the Subaru in the street indicated, next to one of the indistinct apartment buildings. Went one floor up the shabby staircase and rang the bell on the door bearing Oleg's name. No answer. Knocked on the door. Still no answer. So I returned to sit in the Subaru, waiting for the ape to show up.

Eleven P.M., and still no sight of him. I went to the building again and rang the doorbell of apartment number two. A white haired babushka opened the door, cursing in Russian.

"Young man, I'm afraid I'm a little over your age range," she muttered across the aluminum walker she was grabbing. Everything in life is relative. Young to this one, mature to another.

"I'm looking for Oleg Brukhin. Any idea where I can find him, ma'am?"

"Got into problems again? You'll probably find him at his usual hangout." She gave me the address of a nightclub and said don't be as bad to him as a Moscow cop. We're all Jews here, not so?

When I cleared the bouncers and entered this nightclub I couldn't spot him at first among the many gorillas on the fairly large dance floor and the tables around it. A scantly clad waitress led me to a table and brought me the glass of whiskey sour I ordered. I took a gulp of it and then saw Oleg sitting on a high chair next to the bar. I went over and grabbed his shoulder. He turned around, and his talker opened a bit in surprise. Took a split second to kick in my groin with his right foot, then smack me in the face with his left fist. I fell down and he ran out of the dancing hall to a corridor. I got up with pain and ran after him. He opened the ladies' room door , rushed inside and slammed the door shut behind him. I kicked it open and saw him jump outside one of the windows. Ran by some gaping chicks, climbed through the same window and leaped down to the street. He was running faster than a locomotive along the parking meters in a wide boulevard and I ran just as fast after him. Several hundred meters down that boulevard he seemed to be slowing down and I was catching up to him. Then he turned into an alley on the right. I followed close enough to hear how heavily he gaped for air. He jumped onto the iron fence that blocked the alley and started climbing it. I managed to grab his right foot, but he pulled it up leaving his black shoe in my hand. I climbed the fence and leaped after him, felt my left ankle snap and remained on the ground. He was running slowly by that time and   reached the sand dunes bordering the town, then continued walking in the sand, his hands clutching his hips. I stooped up with difficulty, grinding my teeth, and limped in his footsteps on the sand. The night air was heavy with the scent of salt over sea. The sound of breakers hitting the beach thumped in my ears and my temples throbbed wildly. In the light of the full moon I saw Brukhin slump to the sand. I limped a few steps across the dune and stood over him. He turned around to me, took a switchblade out of his pocket and flipped it open in his right hand. I reached for my gun, aimed it to his right leg and blasted the kneecap. He screamed, his agony mingling with the loud noise of the shot, dropped the blade and held his bleeding leg.

"I have civil rights," he cried in my indifferent face.

"Who sent you to tamper with my Alfa?"

"I don't know what you're talking about. Are you mad?"

"As hell. You're gonna get there in about ten seconds, unless you spill it all out. Who paid you to do the job on me?"

"Nobody. Call the paramedics, for Christ's sake."

"I will call them after you spill it out." I kneeled down by him and put the gun to his head. "Christ won't help you. One, two…"

"A guy named Barnes hired me for this. David Barnes,"

I replaced my gun in its holster, took my cell phone out of my pocket and called the paramedics.

19

On the next day in my office I instructed my secretary to call the Registrar of Companies' office, and find out whether BC Development , Ltd has any officer by the name David Barnes. She returned about an hour later, saying affirmative. David Barnes is President of the company. Told her to now call the Registrar of Databases office, get me all personal information about this person. I wasn't too surprised when the picture she laid on my desk about lunchtime turned up to be the same guy I noticed with Seth Frankenheim in Jericho. Now I told my secretary to set an appointment for me with Mira Klein, of the Jerusalem District Attorney's staff, and went off for my habitual lunch with Jonathan Dayan at Taami's.

My cell phone buzzed while I was wiping my Hummus next to Jonathan. My secretary fixed the meeting with attorney Klein at the Public Prosecutor's Jerusalem district office. Got to be there in an hour.

She was sitting on her desk and moved one of her long legs in black stocking in the direction of the chair beside it.

"Sit down. Michael. How is Leora doing these days?"

Leora was a high school friend of hers, going back almost twenty years now.

" I'm sure she's fine, Mira. I'm here for business today. I want you to prosecute this guy."

I placed Barnes's photo on her black skirt. She looked down at it,

"Ordinary fellow. And what has he done to get on your wrong side, Michael?"

"He's just a flunky businessman who tried to kill me a few weeks ago."

"I heard about your accident. How's your companion doing? Heard she's a knockout."

"Forget the niceties. I want you to get this asshole to the crossbar hotel, for life."

"What evidence do you have against him?"

"One Oleg Brukhin, the thug who did the legwork for him, told me Barnes hired him for the job."

"The face in the photograph between my thighs responds to the name Barnes, then? Does he have a first name?"

"David Barnes."

"That's a pretty common name in Israel, as you probably know. Did you have that Russian thug properly identify this particular, photogenic David Barnes as his principal in crime?"

"Not yet."

"And how did Oleg come to make you privy of his association with Barnes for the purpose of your premature dispatch to heaven?"

"He threatened me with a knife, so I used my police issue revolver to pacify him. That apparently convinced him of the great benefit of cooperation with me on that score."

"Even Oleg Brukhin is a human being, Michael."

"Is he?"

"Must you be so visceral? Maybe that's why Leora left you. Maybe she needs a quiet, ordinary guy. She gained a wonderful son, but feels she also lost him because of you."

That truth really hurt. But after a minute of silence I managed to insist,

"Will you or won't you prosecute Barnes?"

"Get real, Michael. You know all of that is not even the beginning of admissible evidence. What's the matter with you? Consider doing things by the book. Next time, get a proper arrest warrant and put your gun away before interrogating a suspect. I'm not going to implicate this Barnes fellow without proper evidence. "

"The law in this country has become a real nightmare, Mira. Say hi to Leora for me. "

I picked the photo off her hot spot and left her office without closing the door behind me.

20

Back in the office I was told somebody else would interrogate Oleg Brukhin. By the time they brought him over to that interrogation he insisted on his right to remain silent and demanded an attorney. A lawyer came and got Oleg released from detention before I knew it. Insufficient evidence to prove he was tampering with my car. The lawyer also said they would sue the police for personal injuries resulting from brutality, assault and what have you. Lots of threats in legalese. When that lawyer escorted the limping Oleg through the corridor leading outside of the station, the thug turned in my direction, exserted his tongue and gave me the finger.

I called two of my deputies to my office. Shut the door and instructed them to see to bugging the offices of BC Development and David Barnes's home. Use state of the art surveillance on Barnes' cell phone, and put a 24 by 7 tail on him. Track his emails too, if possible.

"What about the legality of all this, Michael?" worried one of my deputies.

"Yeah. Of course. Dig up all court orders for these operations, where necessary by law. I want the tapes of all recordings of any and all Barnes's chats and conversations brought to my office. I want to see them every morning on my desk here, along with a full report of anyone he met or spoke with in person, on the phone or by email, where and when. Now go get David Barnes's ass for me."

For weeks on end after that I was sitting back on my chair listening to the mostly boring recordings. Then one morning a particular telephone conversation about meeting in a restaurant to enjoy osso bucco caught my attention. The cell phone call was traced to the small town of Beth-Shean, in lower Galillee, with nothing but a couple Kibbutzim and other agricultural settlements around. Now where the heck could you   find a decent Italian restaurant , good enough for stuck up David Barnes, in that culinary wilderness?

The impossible dinner party was set for that same late evening. I called the police officer trailing Barnes, found his present whereabouts and told him to keep a tight watch. I'm coming over to join him. His name was Boaz and he looked pretty much on top of this boring job, which demands precisely the kind of patience I personally lacked.

Barnes   could   have   been   the   shrewdest businessman, but he was the easiest bad guy I ever trailed. He exited his garage in the passenger seat of a large Mercedes next to a distant cousin of King Kong cramped in the driver seat. I noticed on the other hand that they both looked a bit like observant Jews, what with the yarmulkes they were sporting on their heads. We took off at some distance after them. Traffic was pretty heavy. The Mercedes hit the main road due north through Samaria and we followed in Rona's Subaru. Somewhat south of Nablus the road forked to the northwest and northeast. They made a right and so did we. About 20 minutes later they turned into a sideway. I slowed down a little to let the Mercedes gain distance

on us. The roadsign indicated "Kibbutz Sde Eliyahu" -
No mention of this place in the Michelin guide for
Israel, restaurant section, that I knew of. I drove the
Subaru with enhanced determination to the sideway. As
we entered the small Kibbutz we passed by some
orthodox Jews. The Mercedes was a considerable
distance ahead and turned right again into another
sideway. I saw that this led to a group of three flat
roofed pretty sizeable rectangular structures. I stopped
the car, took the binoculars I carried in the glove
compartment, stepped out by the trees along the road
and zoomed on the complex. The sign above the main
building read "SDA Spice." A spice dehydration plant?

The Mercedes stopped in the large parking lot on
the east side of the plant complex. A bearded man came
out of the main building, and walked over to its
passenger side. He was standing there for a few
moments, obviously talking with Barnes. Then he
returned to the building. King Kong stepped out of the
Mercedes, stretched his huge frame and pivoted around
his heels. I managed to jump behind a tree before he
faced our direction, and Boaz bent just in time behind
some shrubs.

By that time four orthodox Jews came out of
the building, carrying two small wooden crates that
they, in groups of two, placed one on the ground, side
by side. The bearded man who spoke with Barnes also
came out, walked over to a truck and started its engine. I
knew already what these crates contained. Therefore I
stayed out when they brought more of the same, and
watched as the truck stopped right next to these crates.

When the fourth pair of crates lay on the ground, and two of the orthodox guys returned inside, while the other two started loading the crates onto the truck, I returned to the Subaru, restarted its engine, and opened the passenger door for my companion. And when I saw the ninth crate being carried to the truck, I stepped on the gas and drove toward the plant's parking. Gorilla surely heard the wild revving of my engine, because as I was coming he swiftly ran to the truck, and by the time I got beside the parked Mercedes he fired one shot in my direction and the truck took off into the green fields to the north of the plant. I dropped Boaz off by the ninth crate, and he shouted "Police, you're under arrest" pointing his gun at the group of orthodox men. I didn't have time to enjoy this farcical scene as I followed the truck into a field of herbs. My car got stuck in the mud. I jumped out cursing and called the five bearded men to help me get it out, on the double. They complied and after about five minutes it was back on the solid parking lot concrete. But the truck was already several kilometers to the north, and then I watched it join the light traffic on the main road northbound along the Jordan River valley.

I returned to the car and drove it back on the southwest bound sideway, past the center of the Kibbutz and back onto the main highway. I veered north and accelerated as much as I could. A road sign posted by the Ministry of Transport , featuring an air force pilot proudly seated inside an F-16, aptly proclaimed,

"Only he can fly. All others follow the posted speed limits."

I saw nothing of the treasure truck until I came to the foot of the hills just north of Capernaum. The truck was already on top of the road winding uphill. I started negotiating the narrow turns as fast as I could, the setting sun reflecting from the waters of the Sea of Galilee to my right. It took me about twenty minutes to get to the top. By that time the truck was far ahead on the level road, at the small town of Rosh Pina. I floored the gas, but couldn't get much closer to it. Gorilla obviously was doing the same. We zoomed past Kiryat Shmona, into Metula, the northernmost town in Israel. I saw the truck slowing somewhat, then entering the Israeli held security zone in South Lebanon. The road was completely dark now. I turned my long headlights on. But then I heard a submachine gun firing and my front right tire exploding. I stopped the car on the dirt shoulder and stepped out, cursing as I watched the truck race ahead. Another shot hit my windshield. I ducked under the car , took my revolver out of the holster and aimed it out, expecting some Hezbollah gunmen to emerge from the dark. But it was all quiet now. Dead calm. I waited for a few minutes more, then rolled out and lay on my back by the open driver side door, watching the millions of stars blinking in the sky dome above.

An hour later I was back in the parking lot of the Kibbutz dehydration plant. There was nobody there so I drove back to the center of Sde Eliyahu, parked the car and walked over to the Kibbutz communal dining hall. They always feed errant travelers in Israeli Kibbutzim, usually for free. This one resembled a military mess area, but instead of soldiers it had orthodox men and women seated by its long tables. Kosher food, of course. Whatever. It enters   through the mouth and exits the other way... hunger is the best spice. I was hungry. But when I took some chicken soup, put it in a bowl and was just about to gulp it down, someone laid a heavy hand on my right shoulder. I turned around and saw Boaz. He sat down next to me, grinning his gold filled teeth in my face. I grabbed the soup bowl with both hands and gurgled its entire boiling hot content   down my throat. Wiped my mouth with a napkin and commanded,

"Now let's go open that crate, Boaz."

"It isn't here," Boaz said gingerly.

"Where is it, then?"

"I opened it right after you drove off, and saw it was some kind of antique. I called Tiberias police headquarters to send me some men to help guard the thing. They sent two cops, but they had a guy from the Israel Antiquities Authority with them, and he took it. I told him to keep it intact as it may be needed as evidence. He said they would keep it secure in their vaults. Looked   cool, and gave me his business card. Goes by name of Zalman Ganot."

"No shit. Did you have a look at this antique?"

"A small stone box, with some flower shaped ornamentation, and an inscription."

"Did you read the inscription? What did it say?"

"Beats me. It wasn't in Hebrew and it didn't look exactly like English letters, either. It was rather long."

I struck the table in frustration.

"What's the problem, Inspector?"

"I need to know what that inscription is about."

"Call this guy Ganot and ask him. Here, take his card."

"Yeah, right. You should have kept the box until I returned."

" I took a photo standing next to it. I'm sure the inscription can be read, using a loop."

He gave me a Polaroid photo. I put it in my pocket, grabbed him by the shirt and said wearily,

"Let's go home. Boaz. Time to hit the road."

21

Before the cock crowed the next morning I took a loop and examined the Polaroid picture of the bone box, with Boaz standing next to it. I was able to see the letters in the fairly long inscription. They were joined together with no spaces, and when I tried to count there were about 16 or 17 letters. I recognized they were Greek script.

I made myself a cup of coffee and sat staring at this picture for almost two hours. Then stood up, put the loop and the picture in my pocket and drove to visit Rona at the hospital.

She opened her deep black eyes to me and smiled softly as I sat down by her bedside.

"I longed for you, Michael. What have you been up to?"

"I've a lot to tell you. But I know you'd like to hear about this much more than about the action."

I showed her the Polaroid photo,

"This is a picture taken yesterday of one of the ossuaries stolen from the Rockefeller museum. It bears a long inscription in Greek. Can you see it?"

I put the picture a reading distance from her eyes, and the loop in front of it. She asked to move the loop forward a little. Then read slowly,

"Mariamene, who is Mara."

"Who is this?"

"A dead woman whose name was Mariamene and whose nickname was Mara. Why don't you ask

Zalman Ganot to enlighten us about the significance of this ossuary, Michael."

I went to an available computer at the hospital and emailed Zalman a query just about that. Minutes later I had a reply from him, with the following text:

"Magdala Sear Nashia."

I read this new code to Rona.

"And what do you think that means, Michael"

"You know already what that means, so why don't you tell me?"

"You try first."

"Let's see. 'Magdala' means growing?"

"Go on."

"Sear' is hair in Hebrew. But what's 'Nashia?' Wait. Woman? Women? 'growing woman's hair?"

" That's the closest you can approximate from the Hebrew language. But this is Aramaic. It refers to someone working with women's hair. A women's hairdresser."

"Good for her. Now who was this women's hairdresser?"

"I haven't the slightest idea."

I reverted to telling her the events of the last days, but half through my account she fell asleep. I stayed by her side watching her face until dark, and then fell asleep too, on the chair by her bed.

22

Jonathan Dayan paid me a visit several days later at my own office. He just knocked on the door and walked in. He greeted me and I bantered,

"What brings you to my office, Chief Inspector. Usually it's the other way around."

"That matter of the museum ossuaries that ended up in Beirut stirs the highest echelons of the police now, Michael. And even beyond that. Major screw up. We don't want a media circus around this. We've got to get these artifacts back to where they belong. We'll get David Barnes into jail now as quickly as we can. After his prompt conviction in court I expect the Israel Land Administration to reject his company's application to open a museum for exhibiting these antiquities. Matter closed."

" How do you expect to get these ossuaries back into Israel? IDF special operation?"

"Something along that line. We have excellent intelligence in Lebanon. They'll find out where these bone boxes are hidden and send a special commando unit to retrieve them. Don't you worry, we've carried out more difficult operations in that country."

"What do you expect me to do about it now?"

"Nothing, really. You messed up big time, buddy. Shouldn't have acted solo, and we'd have these relics back where they belong without media attention and international ramifications."

"What's so important about these ossuaries? Did the bones belong to some 2000 year old Rabbi and his family? Is that why they were hidden in an orthodox Kibbutz?"

"What difference does it make to you? Lay off these bones and get a life now. Forget about the whole affair. Come, let's go to the cafeteria and have a cup of coffee and some cakes to wash the bitter taste of this thing out of our systems."

At the cafeteria I slumped on a chair by the table while Jonathan went to the counter and returned with two cups of coffee and some cakes.

"Here, Michael. A Napoleon. Your favorite cake."

I took a sip of coffee from the mug and a bite of cream filled dough. Then I closed my eyes, stretched my arms on the table and rested my head on them, my face into the space between my arms and my nose touching the table.

"Hey, Michael, I'm taking a course about Kabbalah. I'm still going there. In fact I'm going there tonight. Why don't you join me? It's called Kabbalah Center, in Hillel street. Rona used to go there, too."

"What time?"

"8 P.M."

I went to the center that evening, and wasn't too surprised to see Leora seated in the classroom. She motioned for me to come over. I did and sat next to her. A few minutes later Jonathan entered the room and sat down next to me.

A thirty something guy entered the classroom, presented himself by name of Jordan, and started talking about a "Tree of Life." God is sitting up somewhere in heaven, emitting blinding light, brighter than a zillion stars. This is the "Shekhina" (presence) of God. A little below the Shekhina, to its right, sits Wisdom, in grey color. On the same level as Wisdom, to the Shekhina's left , sits Understanding, in dark indigo. A little lower in the middle sits Beauty, in yellow color. Still below Beauty, on the right side, sits Mercy, in blue color. On the same level of Mercy, to the left, sits Severity, in red color. Below these two, to the right, sits Eternity, in green color. On the same level of Eternity, to the left, sits Splendor, in orange color. Below these, in the middle, sits Foundation, in purple color, and below purple, in the middle again, sits Kingdom, in olive green, black, red and blue colors.

By this time Jordan began to explain the significance of all these different parts of the Tree of Life according to the Kabbalah. I began dozing off. Leora nudged my shoulder, enrapting,

"Wake up, Michael. You should hear this part."

"Don't you know I'm color blind, Leora?"

I kept my eyes open from that point on, my mind in a different place. Just like the times when Leora used to drag me to the opera. But all boredom comes eventually to an end.

Nevertheless when Leora said next class is in three days, see you here again I nodded consent. For the company, I guess.

23

So we did meet there again a few days later. Jordan entered the classroom and began his lecture.

"Today we'll talk about holy letters. In Jewish society the word is not simply a sound that communicates a mundane meaning. In Jewish culture words in Hebrew, the holy tongue, always had holiness and power, by virtue of being the very Word of God. Hebrew letters have always in Judaism been endowed with deep symbolic meaning and overwhelming, even existential importance. Thus Rabbi Meir, a Torah scribe, recounts how a first century rabbi warned him to be careful with his work, lest by omitting one letter or adding one letter the whole world could be destroyed."

I thought about the letter Taw, and started paying attention to Jordan, much more than I did on the previous class. He was now discussing the meaning of some particular letters, and I learned that the Hebrew letter "Yod" stands for the Ten Commandments and for God; the Hebrew letter "Shin" symbolizes the rule of law; the Hebrew letter "Vav" stands for the nail or the hook. It symbolizes a person with his head in heaven and his legs on earth. Indeed the Vav stands for the connection between heaven and earth, and also symbolizes the divine dimension of time; the Hebrew letter "Aiyn" stands for suffering, for a fountain of life and for universality; the Hebrew letter "Heh," which is silent, stands for the soul. It was added to the names of

Abram and Sarai in Genesis, turning them into "Abraham" and "Sarah," respectively, to signify the elevation of their status by the addition of the silent letter from the Tetragrammaton, the explicit, ineffable name of God.

These five Hebrew letters in turn make the word "Salvation."

Jordan said he would continue to talk about specific letters next session. See you folks then. I walked over to him and ventured,

"This is not something to do with what you spoke about today. But I wonder if you know where the reference to one 'Magdala Nashia,' apparently an ancient lady who was a women's hairdresser, comes from."

"I think I do. It comes from the Talmud. Follow me."

I followed him to the center's library. He took out a volume of the Talmud entitled "Nezikin," opened it and indicated a passage.

"Here it is, Sanhedrin 67a, uncensored version. Sorry but I must go now."

He left and I read the passage indicated, as follows:

"And this they did to Ben Stada in Lydda , and they hung him on the eve of Passover. Ben Stada was Ben Pandira. R. Hisda said: 'The husband was Stada, the paramour Pandira. But was not the husband Pappos b. Judah?' — His mother's name was Stada. But his mother was Miriam, a dresser of woman's hair? (literally "thab tksdn megaddela neshayia"): — As they say in

Pumbaditha, this woman has turned away from her husband."

The bones in the ossuary were   the skeletal remains of a hairdresser who apparently had committed adultery. What the heck does all that mean? Whatever that may be, Rona will certainly be excited to explore it.

I ran to the parking lot and drove the Subaru to the hospital, eager, oh so eager to watch the happiness on her face

24

But when I got to the hospital's reception hall   I was told I can't see Rona, because she's relapsed into coma. I screamed "no" to the full capacity of my lungs and ran back to my Tel Arza apartment all the way from Mount Scopus.

I sagged in my bed in a fetal position, trying to find refuge from the horror, but I couldn't fall asleep. I don't know how long I stayed there, feeling only a miserable wish for extinction. Not to walk, not to talk, not to love, not to think, not to dream. Only to be dead. The cycle of working, talking, seeing people, eating and sleeping again just for getting and spending was exhausted, meaningless and terminated for me. Why should I continue in this cycle? For what purpose did anybody pursue any cycle? There was no purpose to my life, nothing but a deep, uncontrollable longing to make an ending of this painful existence. I should take the same pills Guy took to make me sleep forever. But I can't find the slightest energy needed to do that, starting with going out to get the pills.

I remained inside my dark bedroom until Leora came into the apartment one day, opening the unlocked door. She took one look at me lying in that fetal position and made a hasty phone call. A few minutes later our second son Avi came in. They pushed me gently from the bed, up on my feet and into their car. Then Avi drove to the tree lined Jerusalem neighborhood of Rehavia, into Leora's house garage . They helped me walk the short distance to the guests' bedroom. There I immediately fell on the bed   to resume my quest to escape the world of the living.

But later in the evening Leora and Avi came into the room and asked me to come out and dine with the family. I jerked my limbs unwillingly in the bed. Then from the kitchen I heard our little daughter Daniela calling happily,

"Is Daddy really here? Where is he then, Mommy?"

Her melodic innocent voice restarted my numbing brain, and I recognized the unfairness of my action to her. I could not buy peace by deserting her. So I rolled slowly from the bed, stood up with a sigh and walked with   Leora and Avi back to the kitchen.

As we sat around the table in the dining area, Daniela came over my side and sat on my lap,

"I don't want you to die , Daddy. I don't want you to die like Guy."

"I won't die, Daniela" I made with difficulty and hugged her close against   that aching spot in the center of my chest that hurt so much with mental pain.

"But you're really pretty sick, aren't you?"

I kissed her on the cheek and said no. Go to bed now. She jumped off my knees and left to her room. Leora gave me a reproaching look and said,

"As always you think emotions are something you can just decide about, Michael."

I remained silent and she continued in the same tone,

"You think she, we, didn't also lose a brother and a son when Guy left us? Isn't the sharing of this grief good for us? Don't you think that it would open a deeper contact with Daniela, a healing of her confusion that is so frightening for her?"

"I've felt so alone, especially in the past days, weeks. There is so much grief I don't know where to start, Leora."

"You've pushed so much away, Michael. Try to make room for it all, though I know it seems impossible now. Each grief creates pain around your heart, as the grief over Guy creates over mine. But we shouldn't be so merciless with ourselves. We should try to open our hearts to whatever pain arose there. Start breathing right into it."

" Have you been seeing a shrink? You sound as if you were quoting one."

"Of course, and so should you. Tell him, Avi. Tell your father."

"I don't know," said Avi. "Every round of moaning I hear from you breaks my heart. I remember in the nights right after Guy's death how we all slept in the same room, seeking security in each other's presence. I kept waking up to check that you two were breathing normally. When I returned home from school I would enter surprised and happy to find everyone alive. I was frightened of the near future. Of what will happen to you. At joint breakfasts I was trying to divert Daniela's attention from you, Dad, always resting your head with your eyes closed, your face into your arms and your nose touching the table. But as time passed I realized that I mustn't wallow in sorrow. I would always remember Guy and the beautiful memories I have of him, but I must let him go if I'm to continue with my life. In a sense I became much stronger and mature after his death, though that strength he gave me can never compensate for the joy that passed away."

I stood up, opened the sliding door, exited into the backyard and slumped on a lounge chair, gazing forlornly into the shining half moon drifting silently in the cloudless sky.

25

The sun had replaced the moon as the dominant orb high above me when Leora woke me up, nudging my shoulder. I opened my eyes into the blinding light and closed them again. Then reopened the eyelids slowly and stared into her face.

"Time to get up from this chair, Michael. It's already two o'clock."

I rubbed my eyes. "Is Daniela back from kindergarten?"

"No. She finishes at 2:30."

"I'll go pick her up. Give me the keys to your car."

I went inside the house, drank two cups of strong, black coffee, took her newer model Cadillac and drove it over to the address she gave me. I got there around 2:25, parked by a meter in the street across from the kindergarten's playground, and remained seated in the car.

2:30 come and gone, still she's not here. 2:35; 2:41. Where is the little girl? 2:49. Nowhere in sight. I opened the driver door and exited into the busy street, almost knocking down a bicycle rider. He shouted hey look around before you do that, asshole. I crossed the street, oblivious to the noisy traffic around me, and went to the kindergarten's fence. Some other five year olds were running around the playground, but Daniela wasn't among them. I felt cold sweat creeping on my scalp. Used my cell phone to call Leora. Is she sure this is the right place. She said yes, don't worry, many times Daniela just stays longer in the classroom. I went to the classroom. Nobody there, either. The heaviness in my heart was much worse by now. Called Leora again, panting "she's not here." Leora said don't worry. This is Israel, remember? Not Hollywood. Nobody kidnaps children here. Maybe she went to play at some other kid's home. I dropped the cell phone on the floor and ran out to the street, clutching my chest. I could hardly breathe. But then I saw Daniela standing at the street corner. I started running in her direction and a second later she ran happily to me exclaiming "daddy" and jumped into my arms.

Back at the house Leora said,

"Relax a bit, Michael, will you?"

"I can't talk much now, Leora. My chest hurts so. Maybe I've had a heart attack."

"I don't think so. I think you've had a panic attack. The atmosphere around you hums with fear. Let yourself revert to love instead of fear. Here, read this book, maybe it will help you feel less isolated."

I took the little book she handed me, returned to the lounge chair where I slumbered throughout the previous night, and began to read it.

It was a story of some American psychiatrist that hypnotized a patient who suddenly reveals details of her previous lives. The psychiatrist starts past-life therapy after the patient describes a dozen or so of her previously unknown past lives. The patient recounts that spiritual guides who have been her soul therapists in between lives told her that "our body is just a vehicle for us while we're here. It is our soul and our spirit that last forever." At that point psychiatrist discovers that these guides have specific messages about his dead son. He therefore wrote the book to inform the world about "immortality and the true meaning of life."

I laid the book down, returned to the kitchen where Leora was busy preparing dinner, and sat down on one of the chairs. Her back turned to me, she commented,

"Did you like the book, Michael? I saw you turning the pages quite quickly."

"I wonder if anyone has verified the truth of this story."

"The author is a well respected professional."

"I know you now believe in reincarnation and channeling, Leora. But I don't want to kid myself just to feel better about Guy."

" You think this doctor illusioned just so he could accept his son's death? He was previously himself nonspiritual and scientific."

" I feel my brain physically frying, Leora."

She didn't respond to that and just continued cutting vegetables for the dinner's salad.

"Listen to me, damn it Leora. Listen to me. I'm scared. I really, actually have this boiling sensation inside my head. Maybe I'm turning wacko. Maybe I'll end jumping off the balcony on the second floor of this house."

She turned around and her expression was serious while she examined my face. Then she advised that I should go see a doctor, but I dismissed that idea, saying that won't help. Is the doctor going to return Guy to life, and Rona to consciousness?

The weird sensation inside my head persisted each of the following days. I kept complaining about that to Leora, and she kept replying she's not a doctor.

On or about the fourth day of my stay at Leora's house, a Friday, in the early afternoon, my secretary Dina came to visit me. She said everyone at the office is worried about my long absence. And how do I feel?

I said no sweat, and then asked Dina in low tone if she knew the Bible informs that God is selecting a prophet like Moses every generation from among us Jews, to transcribe His grand designs to the rest of humanity. Dina looked at me with astonishment and confusion, but said nothing. I reasoned,

"If you don't believe me think about Einstein. How did he figure out exactly all these cosmic secrets, in several months at age twenty-six while conscientiously performing the duties of a government official full time inside a Zurich patent office? How did he come up with $E=MC2$? The aliens told him that!"

I hushed my voice even lower and confided,

"Hey listen. You must keep this a secret, Dina. I 'm sure it's not a coincidence that the Bible surfaced among our ancestors. The book of Genesis recounts how some divine giants landed on earth and procreated with humans. This is a mythical reflection of the real event. They were superior beings from some distant galaxy who visited our planet. The prophet Ezekiel actually saw one of their spaceships and described it. But I'm the only one human who knows this today."

Dina   didn't answer. Leora joined us at that point and I realized she's now actually one of these aliens. They've entered her body, but they won't fool me. I changed the subject immediately to office gossip. Then started to question Leora, so that Dina   will understand also that Leora is an alien in disguise. I'm the best interrogator in the country, ain't I? I'll show this particular alien who has invaded Leora's brain how good I am, and he'll stop messing with me, ha ha.

By that point Daniela came into the room with two of her girlfriends, and I thought gee, they won't understand about the aliens, so they'll think I'm cuckoo. But what can I do, must expose this sonofabitch and scare him out of good, gentle Leora. Save her. So I started asking Leora some personal questions that a stranger couldn't know. "She" said these are intimate matters, and why would I want to talk about this when we're already separated. What's the matter with me. I make her worry. She took Dina to the corridor and escorted her to the door, and I heard her begging Dina not to tell anybody about all this. Of course, I realized with terror. They won't have anyone suspect what they're up to. They surely have planted the Bible itself into the Israelites' religion, over 3000 years ago, to best control them with laws built right into it, by ingeniously instilling in the primitive minds of these ancient nomads the myth that it was the Word of God. Now if they find out that I'm the only person who has ever discovered this great secret, they'll first abduct me into one of their spaceships and do the most horrible things to me. They can read my mind of course and wouldn't need to interrogate me, but they'll make sure to set an example of my suffering to deter any future challenge from another human to their absolute authority. And since they know nobody on earth is as brilliant as I am, at this time they'll just want to make sure I'm not around other people to infect them with my knowledge. Isn't that the lesson they meant to convey with the story of Adam and Eve and their severe punishment for the original sin?

I went out to the backyard and sat on the lounge chair. I was pretty terrified. Then our two dogs came to sniff me and one of them licked my cheek. That gesture made me think chances are that these dogs were not invaded by the aliens, and I felt a little more secure to have allies. So I remained outside in the company of my loyal dogs for several hours, until I thought I might as well return home and let the aliens take me. Maybe my negative ideas about them are unfounded. Maybe they're just as nice as these dogs. I stood up to return home, but then saw the alien who has invaded the body of my son Avi walking inside, grasping a long TV cable between his hands. Now I realized that this proves they're indeed going to mistreat me real bad while at the same time choking me with this cable. I must escape from them as far as I can.

26

I walked slowly on my toe tips around the house and exited the yard by the side gate. Then marched quickly to the neighborhood center, entered the local supermarket, looked around to ascertain that nobody pays much attention to me and approached the manager, calling him in a hushed tone,

"Excuse me please."

"How can I help you, sir."

"There are some beings chasing me with real nasty intentions. Can you please call the police to come over and pick me up while I wait here?"

"You do look terrified, sir. Who are these people?"

"Please believe me that I'm not crazy. They are aliens who want to abduct me. If the police come and take me, I would be relatively more secure. Can you please call the police now?"

He went into the market's office area and I thought with great relief that he'll call the police and they'll come any minute now. But instead I saw through the glass window of the office that he was talking to some other man. Then he returned, stood close to me, glanced around us and said quietly,

"I'm afraid I can't do that for you here, sir. But there's a payphone booth outside and you can call by yourself."

Yeah sure, you're one of them yourself, of course. And now that you've told them I'm gonna call the police, your buddies the other aliens will arrive before I know it in a police car, looking like regular policemen, and get me this way, outside where there's nobody to watch them at this time of night. But you can't con me that easily.

I stepped out of the supermarket. Got to find another place of relative safety. I recalled that there was a small private hospital just a few blocks away, and ran over to it. The streets were empty and only a few cars passed on the road next to me. When I came to the corner across from the hospital entrance I stood a few seconds on the pavement waiting for the light to change to "go" at the pedestrian's crosswalk. As the light wasn't changing, I just ran across to the other side and quickly into the hospital's admittance office. There was a woman sitting there. I told her I must be sick, because my son died several months ago and now I'm hallucinating things. I was enjoying my cleverness for inventing this ruse. Now she'll believe me that I'm crazy and put me inside, where the aliens will have a much harder time getting to me. Fooled them again, ha ha. This is working, too. She's calling the warden to escort me to safety. But wait, what's that? See the way this warden walks authoritatively toward me? See the way he looks at me? Damn them, he's one of the aliens himself. I've stepped right into their trap!

I ran out into the night, without looking back, as fast as I could up the wide boulevard. After several hundred meters I could hear no steps of anyone running behind me. The warden must have given up. Probably called to inform them where I was running.

I saw a small coffee shop that was still open, and turned abruptly right into it. The few patrons sitting by some tables looked up at me, and another bright idea struck me. I walked over to one of the tables and panted,

"Please believe me I'm not on drugs or anything like that. This may sound incredible to you, and I know you won't agree to affirmatively do anything right now to save me. But I'm really going to be abducted by aliens. My name is Michael Inbar. I'm a police inspector. If and when I disappear, making you realize this is true, please tell the police, newspapers, TV and radio about this. You'll become the most famous people on earth."

Ha ha, I thought. Now the aliens, who are recording my words of course with their incredibly sophisticated listening devices, will realize that the entire world will soon learn about my abduction. The aliens will reconsider the whole idea. If the world starts investigating my abduction, someone will end up hitting on the real reason for it. Which is of course that I've discovered the big secret of how the aliens have manipulated the minds of most of humanity for the last 2000 years. The aliens will analyze the consequences of my abduction becoming public knowledge, and realize that they're better off in the present situation. Because at this time there's only one person on earth, myself, who has discovered their secret but didn't rat on them thus far. But if they abduct me after I've made sure this will become public knowledge, the whole scheme will be discovered by the entire globe!

A white haired man seated at one of the tables asked me gently for my business card, and then said he's sorry for my predicament and will do everything to help me. He took his cell phone, stepped out to the street and made a call. I couldn't overhear him but I was happy that at least this guy who looks clever indeed was able to understand I'm not crazy. He then went somewhere up the street and returned with a tall policeman. Good, I thought. This is a start for real protection effort against the aliens.

"Protect and serve," I said appreciatively to the policeman. He didn't answer. Serious tough guy.

But at that time Leora's Cadillac came from nowhere and stopped at the curb by the coffee shop, Avi and Leora came out and I realized with horror that the aliens have invaded even more people than I thought. I stirred to stand up but Avi grabbed my shoulder saying come with us, father. And when I resisted violently, the tall policeman walked over to me and grabbed me on the other side. This way they dragged me kicking and screaming between them, pushed me into the backseat of the car, and Avi drove it back to Leora's house while she was sitting next to me stroking my hair.

I ruminated that the aliens apparently have not completely taken over my loved ones, and I relaxed a bit. But when we came in front of the house and both Avi and Leora invited me softly to come in, I refused, thinking that I would still be safer sitting the night out inside the Cadillac. I told them don't worry, this car is so spacious it's about as comfortable as a bedroom. Leora and Avi then left me, and I moved to sit in the front seat, thinking this way it's going to be easier for me to stay on guard. If I were to fall asleep the aliens would come and quickly pick me up to their spaceship. Sometime later Avi came out to the car and said Dad, if you're going to sleep in the car, why don't you lie down on the back seat. I said I like it better this way. He said either come in and go to the bedroom, or go to the back seat. I said I'll stay by the wheel or just walk off to the street again. He nodded in frustration and returned inside the house. From then on I didn't see him or Leora, but the lights in the house were all on.

I sat this way in the driver seat of the Cadillac through the night, my eyelids sometimes closing in fatigue, and then reopening a few seconds later in panic. The wee hours of the night came and went, and pre dawn light returned. I heard a vehicle coming down the street and stepped out of the car. The driver threw the morning newspaper at my feet and drove off. I picked the newspaper up and read the front page headlines. The top story printed in bold characters detailed how Ben Stada had just been executed. I dropped the newspaper in horror on the backseat of the Cadillac and reopened the driver side door, but then noticed something really bizarre incised deep into the concrete driveway and turned to examine it. It was a large X shaped mark tilted sideways, with the lateral arm longer. The mark of the Taw! I closed the Cadillac's driver door and ran away down the street. While I was running several cars came up the road against me, each and every one of them driven by one of the closest people I knew in my life. See how they all heard about me being here, I thought. I jumped suddenly in front of one car, which was driven by my squadron commander in the air force, and nothing happened to it or to me. The car just disappeared in thin air.

When I came down to the busiest street of the neighborhood the genial idea struck me that the best way to ensure that the police will come and take me away, thus providing me some protection from the tenacious aliens, would be to stand in the middle of the intersection and disrupt the traffic there. Either I would be run over and killed, in which case I would escape the aliens and also be rid of my miserable existence, or the police would come in a few moments and snatch me from under my pursuers' noses. An advantage either way.

So I went to the middle of the intersection and stood there. Cars stopped with screeching tires and some rear ended others. Big commotion. One car hit my ribcage with the side mirror as it passed narrowly beside me, and some young bicycle drivers said walk away idiot, someone should beat up your ass. Then the police came and I walked over to them. A man came out of a car stopped at the intersection and said to the policemen he's a doctor. This man is mentally ill. He went over to me and I began screaming things that I don't remember anymore. He handed me a pill and said take this and I pretended to swallow it but instead left it in my hand thinking nobody is going to dope me to make the job easier for the aliens. I may be crazy but I'm no fool.

Then some paramedics came and said come with us, we'll take you to the hospital. I thought yeah sure here they go again trying to con me as if I don't know these "paramedics" are all aliens in disguise. Three big paramedics then dragged me to an ambulance. I was yelling all the time so bad that I felt my lungs exploding, but I was no match against their combined power. They threw me inside the ambulance, it took off and a few minutes later the doors opened again, I was dragged out kicking and screaming to a small room where I was injected with a sedative , then carried along an endless hospital corridor to a large room with three beds, but no other occupants. The door closed on me and I was left there in solitude, still screaming and all covered with sweat. After some time my eyelids became very heavy, I slumped onto one of the beds and fell asleep. Several hours later I woke up briefly, rubbed my eyes in the strong light emitted from the ceiling lamp, made a face to the woman sitting on a lonely chair at the corner of the room who was watching my movements and fell asleep again.

27

When I woke up again I saw that a man had replaced the woman on the chair in the corner. I started screaming get me out of here. An orderly finally opened the door, and said to come with him. I said show me the way out of this ward and I'll go by myself. He said no you have to follow me for a medical test. I said fuck you. He went away for a few minutes, closing and locking the door behind him. He then returned with two other orderlies, one of them pushing a weird looking roller bed, with straps on the sides. They came over to me, two of them held me by my arms and the third injected my right arm, saying this will calm me down. They then stretched me on the roller bed, tied my hands and feet with the straps, and rolled me out to the corridor, all the way down to a large whitewashed room, with several nurses in it. I realized with horror that was it. Now they're going to force some potion down my throat that would torture my innards but not kill me. And then they'll lead me out in the scorching heat of Jerusalem to a high hill, put nails through my hands to a wooden beam and crucify me. I will agonize like that for days and weeks until I die from heat, thirst and exhaustion. They'll make sure to prolong my agony on that cross, that I don't die early by suffocation.

I felt extremely thirsty and uttered "water." A nurse standing by me brought me a glass of water quite rapidly, faking a gentle smile. This is, of course, the torture potion, I thought. But they will force it into me anyway, so why not avoid that additional torture and at least quench my thirst now. I gulped the contents of the glass. Nothing happened to me. I thought maybe this nurse is not one of the enemy. Therefore I pleaded to her to arrange that I'm killed quickly, and not like that. She silently turned away from me with a sad look on her face, and I thought how naive I was to believe that a simple nurse could divert the evil plan of the aliens, who totally control most living things on earth. There was no way out. At that point another nurse came and took blood from my arm and other nurses did other things with my limbs strapped to the bed. I began screaming again. Leora entered the room , came over to me as I lay there with my hands tied to the sides of the bed and stroked my hair, looking very pitiful. He's smeared all over with sweat, she said to one of the nurses. Can't you wash him? The nurse nodded no. And then the orderly came and rolled the strap bed down the long corridor back into the bedroom, Leora walking by my side and holding my hand. I realized that they're first going to conduct these tests on me, to learn what was so special about my being that made me the only living person in the world to have fully understood their evil unrelenting manipulation of humankind. Of course when I die after days and weeks of torture on the cross they will extract my brain for further study of my genius.

Several hours later in my confining bedroom a middle aged man wearing a white lab coat came in and said he's doctor Blumberg the hospital's psychiatrist and how do I feel. I said go away Satan. He said I'm here to cure you, Mr. Inbar, so please help me do that. I repeated go away Satan. This sadistic wolf in the skin of a lamb would get nothing from me but this determined expression of my surgical perception of the reality behind his mask.

By that time I quieted down , to fool them into believing I have accepted my unavoidable fate. I even carried a polite mundane conversation with the woman on duty of the perpetual watch over me seated on that single chair by the corner. Then I told her excuse me, I'm tired but I can't sleep tied up like this. Will you please remove the straps from my limbs. She said I guess that's Okay, came over and untied me. I said thanks and pretended to fall asleep. Several hours passed quietly like that, with the room still fully lit by the high powered lamp fixed in the ceiling.

In the wee hours of the morning I heard her stand up from that chair. I opened my eyelids a slit and watched her pull the door slowly and exit. She closed the door behind her, but forgot to lock it. A few minutes passed in silence. My heart was thumping loudly but I felt there was nobody in the corridor. I stood up as silently as I could from the bed, walked barefoot to the door, opened it elusively and examined the corridor. Nobody there. I stepped out of the room and moved catlike along a succession of closed doors toward the exit. But several doors on, the corridor was blocked by a metal sliding fence. It didn't reach all the way to the ceiling. I started climbing it. But that made much noise around. Seconds later a big orderly emerged from the office by the fence and caught my legs. I tried to kick him off me, but then another orderly rushed out from the same office and grabbed me too. Then another one came running toward us. Among the three of them they forced me on the floor and then hauled me by my arms and legs inside the office. Two of the orderlies held me down on the floor. The third went out and returned pushing the strap bed. They picked me up by the hands and feet, threw me like a sack of potatoes face down on the bed, and strapped the backsides of my limbs to the edges of this instrument of torture. A minute or so later I heard another person coming into the office. I glanced sideways and saw it was a nurse in scrubs holding a long syringe. I realized I'm about to be executed here and now by injection. I screamed in panic as the nurse administered the poison to me and expected excruciating pain to blow the nerves in my entire body within seconds. Then I blacked out.

I woke up the next day with a splitting headache. Leora was sitting by my bed holding my hand. My limbs were again strapped to the bed, but I was now lying on my back.

"I have good news for you" she said. "Rona has come out of coma again."

A few days later I returned to normal behavior and was released from the hospital. The nurses said doctor Blumberg has prescribed an anti hallucinating medicine and gave me a plastic pillbox, instructing to take one pill a day at bedtime. I placed the pillbox obediently in my pocket and followed Leora outside to her Cadillac. She drove me back to my apartment in Tel Arza, escorted me to the door, then gave me a kiss on the cheek and said good bye.

28

Around noon on the next day I went to visit Rona at the hospital. She was indeed conscious and smiled faintly when I entered her room. But she was pale and looked very weak. She did recognize me and we exchanged a few words, then she said she's very tired and I left feeling almost as melancholy as before I first met her.

I returned to my duties at the police district headquarters and resumed performing them mechanically nine to five, six days a week. But I didn't feel better again and was enraged at the happy world surrounding me for being unable to understand me at all. Whatever happened, my colleagues and my friends, real or false, would always drain me with their pragmatic concerns, which were uplifting for the living but nauseating for the dead, who had already irreparably lost all that the material world could possibly offer. Since I had already lost the most precious things in my life, how could I now aspire for other things? And to add insult to injury, the living always forced their pragmatic world on me by rehashing the same painful advice for me to keep up because I had responsibilities. These responsibilities however were actually the precise condition that was the origin of the oppression of my soul, because they were devoid of any corresponding aspirations. Thus every time that my colleagues and friends spoke about responsibilities I felt desperately degraded because they could still have meaningful goals in life while I could not. I was a loser in my own eyes, while at the same time a brilliant inspector in all eyes around me.

One day Jonathan Dayan entered my office and announced,

"I have some real good news for you. The bone boxes are back in Israel."

I didn't show interest, but he continued,

"Listen, Michael. Some operation the IDF launched on this particular account. It involved participation of elite commandos from Sayeret Matkal, Sayeret Tzanchanim and Sayeret 13. They came covertly to a cave near Marj'iyun ,where the stone boxes were hidden, protected by many gunmen. You know there are thousands of unemployed former civil war fighters in that lawless country these days. Many of them were killed, and one of our commandos. Two of the opposition managed to escape with one of the boxes. Our commandos collected all the other relics and returned them intact. From now on they're stored under heavy guard in a new place. I thought you'd like to hear that."

"Sounds like this is indeed some kind of national treasure to you guys at the top. But you won't share your knowledge about what it actually consists of with the underlings, of course. Would you now?"

He didn't answer, and I didn't really care much. But I still asked him where the ninth ossuary was. He said we don't know yet but we'll find out.

29

Rona looked much better on my next visit to the hospital. I felt a minute measure of life knocking at the door of my morbid existence. But she asked,

"What's the matter, Michael. Why are you so grave? My medical condition has improved."

"I know. I'm much better than I was while you were in coma."

She said why, what happened to you. I told her about my psychotic episode, with all the details. She said that must have been terribly frightening. I said you have no idea, but now I'm seeing a psychiatrist, and he says as long as I take some pills he gave me, I will not experience such horror again.

"I wonder why you were so scared about being crucified, Michael. What made you transfixed on that particularly cruel method of execution?"

"I don't know, Rona. I wish I could tell you."

"Something in your subconscious must have scared you about crucifixion. Did you see a movie or hear someone talk about that?"

"No."

"Did you hear something about executions?"

"Not that I recall. Wait, I did read something about someone who was executed."

I recounted how I went to the Kabbalah lessons, and how I read the Talmud passage that young Jordan indicated to me. She said I'd like to read that passage. I went out and got the "Nezikin" volume from the hospital's library, returned to her room, sat down by her bed and read Sanhedrin 67a to her.

"Now that I hear it, I seem to recall that 'Ben Stada' may have been a reference to Jesus of Nazareth in the Talmud," she said pensively.

"But this passage   says Ben Stada was executed on the eve of Passover. I thought that Jesus   had celebrated the Seder dinner the night before his crucifixion. In that case   he must have been crucified on Passover Day."

"I've read that there are actually two timelines for the narrative of the Passion of Christ in the New Testament, Michael. One, of the Synoptic Gospels Mark, Matthew and Luke, indeed says that the Last Supper was a traditional Jewish Seder dinner, celebrated always on the eve of Passover. According to this Jesus would therefore have   been crucified on Passover Day. But the fourth Gospel in the New Testament, the Gospel of John, has a conflicting chronology. It has the Last Supper taking place one night before the Seder. Therefore Jesus would have been taken into custody during the evening of   the fourteenth day of Nissan according to the Jewish calendar, tried by the Roman prefect Pontius Pilate in the early morning of the eve of Passover, and crucified later on the same day."

"I won't ask how you know the New Testament that well, Rona. It's very unusual in this country. But you have this curiosity that I adore about you. Anyway that explains this passage in the Talmud. So it does talk about Jesus?"

"Could be. In that case the Talmud tradition would be corroborating the timeline of the fourth gospel. As a rule the Synoptics represent the preferred version of the Jesus story. But on this question of the chronology of the Passion maybe John has inherited a more authentic tradition. His timing also makes sense, while the timing of the Synoptics makes no sense, but I won't expand on that. I can give you the book where I read this, if you're interested."

I stayed in her company for another hour and then returned to my office. From that day on I was constantly longing for her almost as for Guy and rushed to be with her again every time I could, every day. Only the fear of losing Rona was as intense as my attraction to her.

30

One day while I was thus experiencing the bittersweet sensation of that state of enhanced emotion, Zalman Ganot called me on the phone. He informed me that the 9th ossuary has been flown from Beirut to Geneva, Switzerland, said he has no further details about that and hung up. I took off from the office to tell Rona this item that I knew would fascinate her.

She was extremely interested indeed and opined,

"This must be the jewel in the group, judging by the efforts to gain possession of it. I'm very happy that we know where to look for it now."

She held my hand in hers, and I felt intense pleasure warming my entire being in that contact with her. I looked down at our interlocked hands. How beautiful. But something is peculiar about this picture. My heart leaped and my face boiled. I exclaimed "Rona, you can move!" and shouted excitedly for the nurse.

The nurse came in and I told her Rona has just moved her arm. She called a doctor, who came quickly. He examined Rona, said there's a change in her paralysis, he will have some tests done on her right now, but you have to leave her now, Mr. Inbar. I left for the office and kept calling every second hour about the results. Two days later I was told they now have them. She can move her arms and body, but not walk on her legs. I took the Subaru and speeded to her.

"I want you to get me out of here now, Michael."

"Sure Rona," I answered ecstatically. "Put your clothes on and I'll carry you back home right now."

"You don't need to carry me on your arms at this time, Michael. That can wait for another day. Just call the nurse to help me change from these pajamas, and then you can help me to the wheelchair they already gave me. Right here." She pointed to the corner of the room.

An hour later we exited the hospital to a bright Jerusalem day. A full panorama of the old city, the Temple mount and the gold domed Mosque in its center splendidly arrayed ahead of us, the Mount of Olives to our left, and the garden of the Hadassah hospital where we stood   all greeted us in vivid colors. I helped Rona into the passenger seat of the Subaru, folded the wheelchair and placed it in the trunk, then drove down Mount Scopus heading to Rona's apartment. She opened the car radio filling the space around us with a song of the popular Israeli band Ethnix:

"In your bosom I found solace,
Protecting, giving all,
I never wanted to harm you,
To lose you,
If you only ask I'll take you with me faraway,
Don't say no,
And when the night ends wait for a new day,
It will come, and I'll give everything to you,
Because only love can defeat all the tears,
When the pain subsides I'll keep you with me,
Only love will defeat all the tears."

I felt my eyes swelling, glanced at Rona and saw a tear rolling down her cheek.

31

We used the condominium's elevator to get to Rona's apartment on the third floor. She said why don't you order pizzas to be delivered for us here, Michael. I'm going to my computer to send another query to our friend Zalman Ganot. She drove her electrical wheelchair to her bedroom and came some minutes later with a printout, stating,

"He must be seated by his computer now. Here, read my question and his response."

Her query read: "Hi Zalman, what's the meaning of the Taw mark in the context of Sanhedrin 67a?"

His response was: "Origen, Selecta in Ezekielem 9 MPG XIII 800-801."

"Don't tell me who Origen is, Rona," I blurted in frustration. "But of course you know that, too."

"A   scholar of early Christianity who lived in the beginning of the 3rd century. He was born in Alexandria, Egypt and traveled extensively in the Roman world. He visited Palestine twice before settling here in Caesarea in 231. I have his books. Bring that one from the shelf."

I walked over to her bookshelf, stacked to the ceiling of the living room, took out the volume she indicated, and brought it back to her. She leafed through it in silence, read about five minutes, then said,

"Found, it, Michael. Origen tells how he asked among the Jews about the teachings that had been handed down on the subject of the Taw. The answers which he received are included in the following passage."

She started reading in a clear, steady voice:

"Upon inquiring of the Jews whether they can relate any traditional teaching regarding the Taw, I heard the following. One of them said that in the order of the Hebrew letters the Taw is the last of the twenty-two consonant sounds. The last consonant is therefore taken as proof of the perfection of those who, because of their virtue, moan and groan over the sinners among the people and suffer together with the transgressors. Another said that the Taw symbolizes the observers of the Law. Since the Law, which is called Tora by the Jews, begins (its name) with the consonant Taw, it is a symbol of those who live according to the Law. A third (Jew), one of those who believe in Christ, said the form of the Taw in the old (Hebrew) script resembles the cross, and it predicts the mark which is to be placed on the foreheads of the Christians."

At that moment the doorbell rang. When I opened the door Jonathan Dayan said hi guys, and stepped into the room.

"I thought I'd find you here," explained Jonathan. "I called the hospital and they told me the wonderful news about Rona's improved physical condition and that you took her from there. I need to talk to you, Michael. Actually to both of you. I know Rona well enough to presume that she would want to continue her active involvement in this same case that you were working on before the accident."

"I thought you practically laid me off this case many weeks ago, Jonathan" I reminisced.

"I now want you back on it. We have information that the 9th ossuary was flown to Geneva by whoever brought it first to Lebanon."

"I know that already, chief-inspector. What would you want us to do in Geneva?"

"Find the ossuary and bring it back to Israel."

"We'll go," said Rona enthusiastically.

"You want to join Michael in your condition?" Dayan pondered. "Sure, why not. Go there as soon as possible on a commercial flight. I'll get you the tickets and money for all expenses. When you get there, call Tal Walden at the Israel consulate, who will provide you with logistic assistance. Good bye for now. I know you desire to be left alone."

Jonathan left, the pizza delivery guy arrived, and we celebrated our reunion on hot Four Seasons slices washed down with a bottle of Chianty.

32

We continued our celebration of love on board the El Al Boeing 737 direct flight from Tel Aviv to Geneva. We took two blankets and pulled them over us like a tent, and concorporated passionately in the relative privacy of that improvised device. Three hours later we landed uneventfully at Cointrin Airport in Geneva. We rented an SUV from Avis there and drove directly to the Israeli consulate where Tal Walden was already expecting us.

In the privacy of his consul's office, Walden told us he was already fully informed of this matter. His sources discovered that the private Learjet carrying the ossuary came to an uncontrolled airfield somewhat north of Geneva a few weeks ago. They have no information of the relic's present whereabouts. But just a day before we came he received a cryptic telegram which seems to address that issue. He handed it over to me. This went as follows:

"Best wishes to Detective Argov and good luck to Inspector Inbar. ' I followed 19 by 24 after the first, then at noontime rode the beast to the highest place and saw the Giant's Tooth and the Most New sea' ."

"Can't make anything out of this, Rona," I said and handed it over to her.

"Neither could I," said Walden. "Hope you can decipher it somehow. Call me if you need any further assistance." He handed each of us a business card.

"Where can we find a nice hotel around here?"

"Try 'La Tourelle' in Hermence. My secretary will give you the directions."

We took the directions and returned to our vehicle.

"Now what do you think about this clue, Rona. Seems to me that the author meant us to start deciphering it in the order he wrote it."

"I tend to agree. What's 'the first', then?"

I scratched my head,

"Maybe he's referring to the first ossuary stolen from the Rockefeller, where it all began."

"That would make sense, Michael, What did you say the name on this ossuary was?"

"Matya."

"Maybe that connects somehow with '19 by 24.' But what would that signify?"

"Beats me. Let's go to that hotel first, clear our heads a little."

We crossed the Lake of Geneva on the longest of three bridges connecting the two parts of the city, then proceeded eastbound by the southern coast of the lake. Soon we were driving between fields and vineyards within short distance of the lake in view. We turned left at a sign indicating the Route d'Hermance and were now driving on a path along a small brook. We stopped by a sign indicating La Tourelle and entered a square courtyard within an orchard. A small building stood at the center of this growth, looking like a French chateau in miniature, shaded by tall trees. Rona said I love it, Michael. I took her wheelchair out on the pebbled ground, unfolded it quickly, settled her in it and into the small reception office we went. Yes, they had a room for us. Second floor, but there's an elevator.

The room was well lit, with several windows and a French door, its wooden frame painted in blue, opening to a small veranda touched by outgrowth of an ancient oak tree.

A Bible lay on the night table by the right side of the bed. Rona picked it casually and leafed absently through the pages. Then she smiled and said,

"I think I know what 'Matya' refers to. Let's see, 19 by 24. Here it is. New Testament, Gospel of Matthew, chapter 19, paragraph 24."

"Read it now, will you Rona?"

"Jesus said to his disciples 'Again I tell you, it is easier for a camel to go through the eye of a needle than for someone who is rich to enter the kingdom of God'."

"The author says he rode the beast, Rona. That may indeed be a reference to this passage. He 's a rich man riding a camel, then? An oil rich Arab Sheikh from the Gulf emirates, perhaps. But no, these votaries of Allah would certainly not use clues based on passages from the New Testament."

"Whoever this rich man is, the next nut to crack is the high place. That usually refers to holy sites. What holy sites do they have around here. Not many, I believe. Certainly nothing famous."

"But maybe he's just referring to high grounds somewhere. I got it, Rona. I think I got it. This country does have high places. Indeed the highest places in western Europe. The Alps."

"Good point. And the highest mountain in the Alps is the Mont Blanc. Actually it's very close to Geneva. I remember I was here once in the summer, and saw it towering massively in the south."

"Bingo. I'm hungry now. Let's go out for dinner. We're in gourmet territory."

"Right. Dress up my love, and let's sample French food, Swiss style"

So we wound up dining at a culinary high place with terrace on the water in the small village of Hermance, just before the French border, with its old streets, harbor and beach. After which Rona said let's return to the charming hotel room, and the rest of the night will depend mostly on our capacity for adaptation, creativity and passion for each other. I can't tell you how excited I am to spend this night with you at a place like this.

33

    The skiing resort of Chamonix is located at the foot of the Mont Blanc Massif, about sixty kilometers southeast of Geneva, and it took us fifty odd minutes to drive there in our rented SUV on the next morning. We parked the SUV in a public parking at the center of town and walked outside to a winter wonderland.

    The streets were crowded with tanned people sporting the latest winter fashion garb carrying skis on their shoulders and negotiating the glistening ice covering some of the pavement amid white piles of snow all around us.

    We saw many skiers entering a cable car station and I followed them into it, while Rona remained outside. I walked over to a picture board on the wall by the ticket counter. It described the history of this cable car, which until the 1940s was the longest in the world, linking the center of Chamonix, at 1035 meters above sea level, in two spans, with a peak called Aiguille du Midi at 3842 meters. I reread this information and exited in stride toward Rona. She smiled, raised her hand and indicated the cable car climbing to a sheer rock in the sky high above the southern outskirts of Chamonix.

    "I know, Rona. Aiguille du Midi- The Needle of Noon. The cable car is the beast."

"Your French is good, Michael. Needle of South or of Noon. Let's ride the camel to heaven through the eye of the needle."

We rode the cable car in two stages, traversing a large glacier before rising vertically up the North Face of the mountain. We exited at the top station into a terrace humming with skiers all wearing fashionable sunglasses in the bright sunlight, reflecting the stunning panorama of blazing white mountain peeks that surrounded us.

"How beautiful," exclaimed Rona.

"Incredible. Now let's look for the Giant's Tooth. It's probably the name of one of these mountain summits."

I walked over to the metal fence surrounding the terrace. There was a telescope there with a panoramic picture, detailing the names of the different peaks. I read through all of them but couldn't find any reference to a "giant," a "tooth" or a combination of the two words.

At that moment someone grabbed my waist with inhuman force from behind and threw me up and over the fence. I stretched my right arm backwards and managed to hold the railing, my back against the bare steep rock and my legs dangling in empty space 2760 meters above the valley floor. The view stretching before and below me was certainly even more spectacular in that position, but I didn't have neither the presence of mind nor the time to enjoy it. Rona was screaming "help" behind me, and seconds later many arms grabbed me and I was pulled back over the fence. I stood up, examined the faces anxiously staring at me but didn't recognize anybody. My assailant had probably taken off right after he catapulted me into the air. I recalled the joke about the parrot flying outside the passenger jet and broke the tense silence around me in laughter. Then I blurted,

"Hey Rona. While lifting my head to the sky over the fence where I was unceremoniously dispatched I noticed there's another terrace on this rock's highest elevation. Must be spectacular. Let's go up there."

There was indeed an elevator inside the rock that took us another 42 meters to the top. We exited to the terrace and reexamined the crests   glistening in the sunlight in a semi circle below us. There was another couple enjoying the view there. Apparently tourists like us, with no skis. Rona asked them,

"Excuse me. Are any of these peaks called 'Giant's Tooth'?"

"Not that I know," the man answered in American. But the woman said in English with a heavy French accent, stretching her right arm and indicating another peak, just southwest of the E shaped face of the Mont Blanc,

"See that rock tower below that mountain? The mountain is called Grande Jorasses, the ridge leading to the tower is called Arete de Rochefort. The tower itself is named Dent du Geant."

"So Giant's Tooth is that rock obelisk below. Now what the heck does that have to do with a sea, Rona? Wait, don't tell me. The riddle refers to a Most New sea, in capitals. Most New is therefore a sort of name. And here I'm lost."

We gazed in silence at the white scenery all around us for the good part of the next half hour, then Rona exclaimed,

"It's a term in Greek, Michael. 'Pleistos' which means most, and 'ceno' which means new."

"Great. And where does that take us, girl?"

"To the Pleistocene, 1.8 million through 11,000 years ago."

"Got you. The great ice age. Now let's find the particular area called sea of ice. No bones about that."

"I know where that is," the American tourist said indicating a valley glacier descending like a river of ice between the mountains. "It's one of the longest glaciers in western Europe. And it's formed by a confluence of the glacier du Geant, which you can see below the Dent du Geant, with another glacier. Famous 'Mer de Glace,' down there."

34

We rode the cable car back down to the center of Chamonix and went to lunch in a restaurant across the street featuring traditional food from Alsace, where we both consumed good portions of Choucroute. I asked the waiter how to reach the glacier, and he said it's easy, take the cog-train from the Place de Mer de Glace a couple blocks from here.

We boarded a charming little red train from the square the waiter indicated and it ferried us up to a site called Montenvers. It was an easy walk from there to the glacier.

We stood before a panoramic view of the valley glacier for several minutes, wondering whether we had decoded the email correctly. Then I saw a sign indicating a grotto in the glacier. I escorted Rona on her wheelchair back to a small café at the Montenvers site, returned alone to the glacier and walked over the hard, crevassed, rolling ice field to the entrance of the grotto.

It was an artificial grotto cut in the ice. Inside it I found a large crystals gallery cut in the rock. There were a few other people in there, all looking pretty harmless. I walked around the grotto, back and forth, examined the crystals and the glass wall, but couldn't see anything other than frozen H_2O and pieces of rock. I was about to leave when a small ball of yellow paper came flying from outside the grotto through the entrance carved in the millennial ice. The ball hit my forehead, fell back on the ice floor and stopped cold seven feet between me and the entrance. I reached for a gun in my jacket. But I didn't have any gun of course. I wasn't in Israel any more. I picked a large piece of ice and threw it in the direction of the entrance. There was nobody there now, but a woman standing next to me stifled an alarmed cry, fixing my face with widely open blue eyes, her hand over her mouth. I walked toward the living daylight, bent down and picked the yellow ball of paper, crossed over the ice mass and returned to the café. Rona was seated on her wheelchair by a small plastic covered table, sipping from a diminutive cup of espresso. I walked over to the table, sat down by her side, and handed her the ball of paper. She opened it, read a moment or two, and handed it back to me. I removed my sunglasses and read the following:

"Two taken on the rock, and the substitute in the place of exile gave the linen to the archpriest who wrote sorrow on the bosom of the earth but preserved it in presence of the black angel of death in the distant time of the Seventh Warrior reflected in the mirror, who dwelt at the knight's abode later destroyed by the earthly Satan. But the cloth is not in Tau?"

I put this literary marvel in my pocket, and muttered,

"Let's go baby, I need some rest. I saw a sign indicating a tunnel to Italy, and that's probably the best route away from the tourist crowd. Too many people here, too much talk. We'll find a private place where we can concentrate on decoding this unearthly puzzle. Amen."

35

Twenty odd minutes later we were driving inside the Mont Blanc tunnel, longest in the world, after we paid the passage fee of 90 French Francs at its northwest entrance. We drove through the 11.6 kilometers of the tunnel in silence. When we emerged into the daylight again and were waived through the French-Italian border Rona indicated a welcome sign to Courmayeur, and said Michael please take a left into the town's center. I said isn't that another ski resort? She said indeed it is, but I know a fairly quiet place here that I'd love to visit with you. Ever eaten in a restaurant founded several centuries ago?

Casa de Fillipo was located in a two story chalet style house. We entered through the open door and stood on a small landing area below a straight stairway leading to the second floor. Baskets of fruits and nuts hung on the steel railings of the stairway. A sign indicated the restaurant on the second floor, but there was no elevator or any device to facilitate the access of handicapped persons to it. Rona pointed out,

"The owners live in an apartment opposite the restaurant."

I went up the stairs, knocked on the door to the apartment, and a middle aged man responded quickly. He descended with me to carry Rona on her wheelchair up the short stairway into the small rustic dining room of the restaurant. It had six or   seven simple cloth covered tables, some flanked with short benches and some with single chairs. We sat down to one of the latter, and a young waiter came and put a selection of cold meats and cheeses on our table. I asked him in English for the menu, and he responded in Italian something like no parlo inglese. Rona said in Hebrew they don't have a menu here, they just tell you what you can eat. It's a very large selection of specialties of this region called Val d'Aosta. She turned to the waiter and told him in French we'll have the Polo a la Caciatore as main course. He turned back to the kitchen and she said now let's peruse that clue again. We can discuss it freely in the quiet here, and the waiter certainly wouldn't understand our Hebrew. I took the yellow paper from my pocket and laid it open on the table cover. Read the piece again and opined,

"I believe we should first try to find the period this refers to. It talks about a 'Knight's abode.' That would indicate the period of chivalry. It also talks about something preserved from the black angel of death. Maybe this refers to some serious epidemic. A plague?"

"I think you've got it. Many plague epidemics struck Europe up until the Twentieth century. Come to think of it, the most devastating plague epidemic killed a third of the population of Europe in the middle of the Fourteenth century. That was indeed a period of chivalry, especially in Western Europe."

"I know that. The Black Death. And this message refers to that same epidemic when it says something was preserved from the 'black angel of death.' Now who's 'the Seventh Warrior reflected in the mirror,' and what's 'the distant time' he lived in? Whoever feeds us with these clues obviously thought we must pinpoint the precise date."

"I'm not sure about that. Since he's already indicated the period of the Black Death. That plague hit Europe in the late 1340s through the mid 1350s. I think there's a more subtle reference here to something else."

I said "and what's this thing about 'Tau'? Maybe a reference to the Taw mark?"

At that point the waiter returned and put some additional large plates of various regional antipasti on our table. I sampled all of them and liked especially the marinated balls of Mozzarella. I commented on that, and Rona passed and said she thinks the Seventh Warrior is the central personality in a book of history she's read several years ago, entitled <u>A Distant Mirror</u>. She needs to get this book now, but we certainly won't find it in this little skiing resort. She proposed let's drive to Turin, a major city in this part of Northern Italy. We'll go to a bookstore there. I said why not return to Geneva, probably closer, and she said because I have another hunch on this, again having to do with the New Testament. But I may be wrong. So let's just finish our lunch here and take the motorway to Turin, about 140 kilometers away.

36

We exited the motorway at Turin by mid afternoon in the direction indicated to reach the center of this capital of the Italian car industry. Parked the SUV at a small rotund square next to a long arcaded boulevard, which according to the signs was Via Roma. I took Rona's wheelchair out of the backdoor of the SUV, rolled it up to the passenger side door, opened it and settled Rona in it. Put some of the change I received previously at Casa de Fillipo into a parking meter and off we went to the shaded sidewalk flanked with arched openings   showing the busy vehicle traffic on the street. This arcade reminded me of the inner yard entrance to the Rockefeller museum, where it all began.

We walked along this elegant shopping street, looking for a decent bookstore. But it was all about the latest Italian fashion. Then we came to a large rectangular square, named Piazza Castello, featuring a palace, a church and another palace. Rona said this is all Eighteenth century style, and isn't it impressive? I said yeah but where's the bookstore. We entered a small café, ordered espressos with Italian Tramezzini, and ate these delicious local sandwiches by the counter while sipping the strong coffee. When we enquired about a bookstore the barman indicated farther down the Via Roma and said in good English that we'll find one in the Palazzo Dell'Academia della Scienze.

When we finally got to the bookstore, Rona picked up a volume of the New Testament and the history book she'd mentioned earlier. Then she leafed through a city tourist guide. Suddenly she stopped and handed me the color brochure, indicating,

"Look Michael. I thought that 'Tau' in the message was indeed a reference to the Taw mark, as you suggested. But this says 'Tau' is a word in ancient Celtic, meaning 'mountains' and is the origin of the name of this very city. Now let's check these books out and find a nice hotel, because we're definitely in the right place."

37

We drove the SUV a few blocks to another square, named San Carlo, tried a few hotels in the area and checked into the Baroque style Grand Hotel Sitea. I opened the French door of the room we got and we both sat on the lounge chairs in the small balcony facing a rectangular backyard lined with red roses. I took the cryptic message out of my pocket and placed it on the glass plate of the small round table between the chairs, and Rona put her two volumes on it.

"Okay, now what is it in the New Testament that brought us here in the first place, Rona?"

"Listen Michael, I believe that a certain passage in the New Testament, coupled with information in this book detailing the history of the Fourteenth century in France, may point to the famous Shroud of Turin."

"You mean that fake cloth bearing an image believed to be a picture of Jesus, and therefore his actual burial shroud? But that's a preposterous proposition."

" My proposition at this point is not about the logic of that idea or about its scientific validity. Real or fake, this message on the piece of yellow paper directs us to that relic. Start by listening attentively to the details of this passage, Gospel of John, 20:6-7. It follows an account of how two of Jesus' disciples entered his tomb. The primary burial tomb where Jesus' body was placed shortly after his crucifixion." She opened the New Testament volume and read aloud:

"Simon Peter came and went into the tomb. He saw the linen wrappings lying there, and the cloth that had been on Jesus' head, not lying with the linen wrappings but rolled up in a place by itself."

"But what makes you think that our message is talking about Simon Peter, Rona."

"The message mentions a rock, and that's a clear reference to this same famous apostle. Jesus said to him once that he should be called Cephas, which is Aramaic for rock."

"Wait Rona, wait. If there was a second cloth that had wrapped Jesus' head, how could the Shroud of Turin possibly be the real thing? To the best of my recollection this relic is made of one piece of cloth, which shows a full body upfront, notably including the head."

"Great observation, and it's actually the subject of the second sentence in the yellow paper message here. But let's discuss first things first. We have an indication that this is all about the wrappings put on Jesus' body after his crucifixion. Now let's proceed to the next clue in the message."

"I know, Rona. The 'substitute' is a Pope. The Popes are considered the substitutes of that same apostle Peter, who was the first leader of the Christian community in Rome, executed under the Roman emperor Nero."

"Correct. And what's the 'place of Exile'?"

"Piece of cake. That refers to the exile of the papacy from Rome to the city of Avignon, France. So now you have a Pope supposedly giving the object of the message, which is   presumably the actual death shroud of Jesus, to an archpriest. And who's this character?"

"I believe we have to study this history book for that."

"A Distant Mirror? what makes you believe you'll find the answer here?"

"Because the central personality in this book was one Enguerrand de Coucy, the Seventh."

" He's the 'Seventh Warrior,' with some etymological extension of the French language. Still I wouldn't be sure on that basis."

"Neither would the author of the clue. That's why he inserted the additional information about the Knight's abode that was later destroyed by the earthly Satan."

"The knight's abode is probably a medieval castle. Does that refer to the castle of the Seventh Warrior, this Enguerrand de Coucy fellow?"

"I believe so. That same castle was destroyed by the German army during the First World War."

"Got you. Don't tell me- 'the earthly Satan' is Adolf Hitler, who fought as a corporal with the German army in that great war, on the French front. That does point to your book, then. Coupled with the words 'distant' and 'mirror' appearing literally in the text. Now we have to find in the book who the archpriest was, and why a Pope would have given him a supposedly important relic during the ten or so years in the middle of the Fourteenth century when the Black Death was devastating western Europe."

Rona opened the book, and I sat there quietly enjoying her curiosity. Twenty minutes passed in silence and then she said,

"Here it is. I'll just tell you that a previous paragraph here details that military companies roaming the countryside at the time were said to 'write sorrow on the bosom of the earth' just like this message quotes. Now let me read the pertinent parts of the real important paragraph to you:

'The most notorious of the French was Arnaut de Cervole, a noble of Perigord called the 'Archpriest'...in the anarchic months of 1357 (he) made himself commander of a band which called itself frankly enough 'Societa dell' acquisito'...the band grew to an army of 2,000 and the Archpriest into one of the great evildoers of his time. In the course of a raid Cervole launched through Provence in 1357, Pope Innocent VI felt so insecure in Avignon that he negotiated for immunity in advance. Cervole was invited to the papal palace, 'received as reverently as if he had been the son of the King of France,' and after dining several times with the Pope and Cardinals, was given pardon for all the sins-a regular item in the companies demands-and the sum of 40,000 ecus to leave the area."

"So the message author suggests that the same Pope Innocent VI may have given the Shroud of Jesus, along with the money, to this powerful bad guy? But this book says nothing whatsoever about a shroud."

"Indeed the book doesn't mention anything like that at all. But you must admit this does make sense, especially if the Pope knew the Shroud was a fake, with no real meaning to Christianity. That's exactly what the author of our message infers, in the second sentence, where he stresses that the cloth is not in Turin."

"Wow Rona, that does all seem to fit, so we got everything in the message. But I'm getting confused. Let me recap and put everything in order."

"Go ahead."

"Two taken on the rock, and the substitute in the place of exile gave the linen to the archpriest who wrote sorrow on the bosom of the earth but preserved it in presence of the black angel of death in the distant time of the Seventh Warrior reflected in the mirror, who dwelt at the knight's abode later destroyed by the earthly Satan. But the cloth is not in Tau?'

1. Two taken on the rock are the two pieces of the burial wrappings of Jesus;
2. The rock is Peter the apostle;
3. The substitute is the Pope;
4. The place of exile is the papal palace in Avignon;
5. The Pope who gave the linen is Pope Innocent VI;
6. The archpriest who wrote sorrow on the bosom of the earth is Arnaut de Cervole; the linen was given to him.
7. But the cloth is not in Tau? Means that the author tells us the Shroud of Turin must be a fake.

Summing it all up, the author of the message to us suggests that Peter the apostle would logically have taken the two separate pieces of burial wrappings of Jesus to Rome; that these wrappings could have been taken to Avignon when the papacy moved there; that Pope Innocent VI could have given a piece of cloth which supposedly covered Jesus' body to this evil French warlord in or about 1357, to buy his mafia style 'protection'; and that the same piece of cloth has ended up in the Turin church, which now exhibits it as the venerable Shroud of Jesus. But the author believes the Shroud is a hoax that same Pope played on the villain, because it doesn't fit the New Testament's explicit description of not one but two burial wrappings."

"You got it, Michael. We'll visit that church tomorrow-- now let's go to dinner. I love Italian food over Chianty."

38

We did go to that church early on the next day, but could find nothing there to advance our search for the missing ossuary. Neither in the Church of the Holy Shroud, nor in the crypt where the Museum of the Holy Shroud was.

In essence the Museum traced the various stages of the history of the Shroud and the scientific studies on its image. The center piece of the museum was of course the rectangular exhibition capsule made of glass featuring the Shroud. It was located in the middle of the gallery under arched supporting columns that looked like medieval structures and reminded me of the architecture of the library at the Rockefeller museum in Jerusalem.

The place was packed with visitors, but after a few moments of pushing and shoving over the few meters of distance, I managed to get a relatively close look at the contents of the glass capsule, culminating in an astonishing three-dimensional image of the Man of the Shroud processed in 1978 from pictures taken of the famous piece of cloth. I perused the image and its capsule carefully but couldn't see anything there that would evoke a further clue on my search for the ossuary. Same goes for the other parts of the exhibition, where considerable space was devoted to explanation of the studies of the Shroud's fabric, its weave, the microscopic traces of pollen, blood, aloes, myrrh, agonite found in the cloth, forensic tests, the imprint of coins left on the Shroud and iconography analysis. A special section was devoted to the history of the Shroud and its worship, documented by drawings and coins. I saw the casket used to transport the Shroud from France to Turin in 1518. This was open and I could examine the casket's inner and outer parts. Nothing there. I also examined another silver casket used to preserve the Shroud during many centuries. Same negative result.

By that time I was separated several meters from Rona, who couldn't get as close as I did to the various exhibits with her wheelchair among the multitude of visitors. Find anything? She asked. I said no. There's nothing there. I don't believe there's a point in watching their multimedia displays designed to help visitors to visually understand the evolution of scientific research of the Shroud, including the eidomatic studies carried out on the image by computer. Neither is our investigation likely to gain anything from detailed information about the Brotherhood of the Holy Shroud, the owner of this museum. Unless we wanted to learn about how to make tons of money from nothing of real substance.

"Amazing, isn't it Michael, how many millions of visitors flock to this museum to watch a piece of linen that all scientific evidence consistently proves to be a forgery. Since the author of the cryptic message that brought us here knew that, too, it wasn't very considerate of him to waste our time. I believe someone is just leading us on a wild goose chase."

I struck my forehead with my palm and spattered,

"I think I'm certain now who this person is, Rona. He did send us on a goose chase, but he also wanted to make a point. Let's go away from the crowd here and plan our next steps."

"Right. I think we should take a day or two off to refresh our bodies and clear our minds. Milan is about 130 kilometers from   Turin. Let's drive there, a mere one hour on the same motorway we came from Courmayeur, in the opposite direction."

39

"I still believe the author of that clue may have been trying to convey a more meaningful message to us, Michael," opined Rona while we were driving at 130 km/h on the busy motorway about halfway between Turin and Milan.

"Like what do you mean?"

"I believe the word 'Tau' has a double meaning, the second deeper than the first."

" You mean it's a sort of double entendre?"

"No, " she smiled. "Not a sexual sort of double meaning. It does refer to the city of Turin, but it's also the name of a specific letter in the Greek Alphabet."

I wasn't really paying much attention to this chat because I was watching a large black Mercedes in my rearview mirror, that I'd noticed driving at some distance behind us since we boarded the motorway on-- ramp at Turin. I accelerated the SUV and said casually,

"So? What's the point?"

"The point darling is that the Greek letter Tau is the equivalent of T in Latin, and of the letter Taw in Hebrew."

The black Mercedes was accelerating behind our SUV and was now following us at a distance of about three car lengths. I knew I couldn't possibly outspeed it and there was no off- ramp close enough to escape into. I told Rona to hold tight to her seat and drove the SUV a bit closer to the shoulder of the motorway. The Mercedes was now tailgating us at less than one car length. I recognized the driver as the same gorilla who was driving that van with eight ossuaries I had chased into Lebanon. He must have been enjoying the reversed roles now. I held the wheel steady, preparing the next move. The shoulder was hardly the width of our SUV, but it would do. The Mercedes leaped forward and to the inner lane, its right front bumper aiming directly at our left rear bumper. No sir. I wasn't going to flip over again with the same precious passenger. I steered slightly to the right, straightened the SUV inside the shoulder, and slowed gradually while the Mercedes overtook us in a roar and merged into the eastbound traffic on the motorway ahead of us.

"Who was that?" said Rona.

"Probably the same monkey who threw me over the fence on the Mont Blanc," I answered while returning to drive on the outer lane of the motorway to Milan. "You mean that the Tau may have had the same symbolism for ancient gentiles as the Taw had for Jews?"

She didn't answer that one right there on the motorway. At which time I took the motorway exit marked Milan centro cita, parked at the curb of the huge square by the famous Duomo and she said let's go find a hotel with a computer and I'll email our mentor ex machina Zalman a query about the symbolism of the letter Tau in the Greco-Roman world.

On that note I helped Rona out of the passenger seat into the wheelchair and we went out to the large rectangular piazza throbbing with people everywhere, some bustling their way to offices from lunch breaks, others strolling around and window shopping the stylish stores under the two long sides of the square, which were actually arcaded buildings. In the center of the square stood an equestrian monument featuring a figure of some important looking fellow as he reins a horse. Several blocks away from the square we spotted a modern looking hotel with a glass and stone façade, decorated with plants. Rona said let's try this one and we entered a lobby featuring arched ceilings, black and marble flooring, marble pillars and more decorating plants. Rona said let's check in and so we did, landing in a modern style guestroom with wood panels, patterned bedspreads and carpets, work desk and a minibar. I turned the television on for her , returned to the lobby, found the hotel computer and emailed Zalman the query Rona requested. I looked around and saw no sign of gorilla man, then took the elevator back to our room.

Rona flicked the TV off when I reentered and proposed we take a joint shower. I remained silent for a few seconds and she said don't worry about the technical details of this suggestion. I figured that one out already. I can sit and you can stand over or sit by me. I then learned once more everything can be possible and exciting for us when we really want it.

An hour later we exited the hotel lobby, returned to the Piazza del Duomo and entered an extravagant art deco style glass topped, barrel vaulted tunnel called Galleria Vittorio Emanuelle. It was actually a lively, noisy and colorful shopping mall, teeming with life and featuring many bars and restaurants. We sat by one of the tables that spilled from a restaurant, ordered cappuccinos and tramezzini and passed an hour or so people-watching. Then we returned to the SUV parked at the huge square, drove it to the garage of the hotel and took the elevator to the lobby. I walked to the hotel computer, checked my email, saw a message from Zalman, which was relatively long this time so I printed it, returned to Rona's wheelchair and handed it to her. She looked around, said let's go to a table in the far corner of the lobby, behind the supporting column there. As we got there I sat dutifully across the table from her. At that point I glimpsed a huge figure entering the lobby from the street. I moved my chair behind the concrete column closer to Rona and she read the message,

"According to the early church leader Tertullian 'the Greek letter Tau is the very form of the cross.' He writes that 'at every going in and out, on our clothes and shoes, when we bathe, when we sit at table, when we light our lamps, on couch, on seat, in all ordinary actions of daily life, we trace upon our foreheads the sign' that in Tertullian's Greco-Roman world was the Greek Tau, and it had especially to do with the cross on which Jesus died. In fact the equilateral cross used widely in the Hellenistic church corresponded in shape to the Greek letter Tau and the Latin letter T, and was therefore known as the Greek or Tau cross."

"All that mumbo jumbo boils down to the author of the message who sent us to the Shroud of Turin signaling that he holds an ossuary marked with a symbol of great theological significance not only to Jews of antiquity, but also to their gentile Christian contemporaries. Correct, Rona?"

"I think you're right. Moreover, I understand this mark actually indicates the Messiah."

I said got it. Peeped to the lobby and it was empty. Said I'm tired darling, let's go back to the room. Once there I double locked the door from the inside, took my gun out and laid it on the night table, opened my arms to her and said come on baby. She remained in my arms throughout the night, while I kept my eyes slit on the door, and my ears open to the elevator in the corridor.

40

At 5:18 in the morning I rolled out of the queen size bed, stood up, dressed as quietly as I could and went down to the lobby. The restaurant was closed but I spotted an automatic coffee maker, dropped some lire into it, got a paper cup filled with hot cappuccino, sipped a bit and exited to the street holding the cup in my hand. I walked up the Via Flavio Baracchini, the street to which the hotel entrance opened, examining all the vehicles parked along the curb. Then I went back down the opposite side of that street, doing the same. Next I turned into some other side streets, which were all equally deserted at that hour. Finally I saw it. The black Mercedes that had almost knocked me off the motorway on the previous day. I went to the rear of the Mercedes, looked around and saw nobody, took the ball of yellow paper with the cryptic message, stuck it deep into the car's exhaust pipe, then drank up the rest of the coffee from the paper cup and stuck it into the same pipe, open side covering the yellow paper ball. Looked around again and saw only one grey swallow picking at a cub of corn on the pavement. I then walked briskly back to the hotel lobby, checked out, returned to our room, woke Rona up and asked her to prepare to leave. Twenty minutes later we were seated in the SUV inside the hotel garage. She asked where are we going now and I said Vaduz, Lichtenstein, baby. Started the engine and drove out to the drowsy streets, followed the directions to Como, and in about fifteen minutes we were on the main motorway northbound to Switzerland.

Twenty- five minutes later, when signs for the Como exit first appeared about a hundred meters ahead of us, Rona proposed let's go to Como for breakfast, darling. I took the off- ramp indicating city center. Nobody was following us. Ten minutes later we parked the SUV a little outside the center. And two minutes after that we were strolling down cobbled pedestrian streets winding their way to the south shore of the large Como lake past parks and many cafes. Most of these were still closed at this time of early morning. But when we got to a large   square dominated by a splendid cathedral, we saw a waiter arranging tables in a bar directly across from the cathedral. We crossed over the piazza and sat down by one of the tables, ordered cappuccinos and tramezzini, and Rona exclaimed,

"How romantic, Michael. Look at the façade of the Renaissance-Gothic Duomo. Fifteenth century. The statues include two of Como's most famous sons, Pliny the Elder and Pliny the Younger, who were among the most important scholars   in the first century. One of their writings, about the geography of northern Africa and western Asia, includes a detailed description of Judea, the Dead Sea, and even a reference to the sect of the   Essenes. The same sect   most experts believe authored the Dead Sea Scrolls, including the Great Scroll of Isaiah, which we found bearing the Taw marks to specifically indicate eleven passages, expressing deep messianic expectations."

"All that is very interesting, Rona. But maybe we should now hit the road to Vaduz."

"Good, I'm happy this hunt for an ancient burial device seems to revive you, Michael the Zombie. In fact one of Pliny's essays, about anthropology and human physiology, even expounds about revival of people pronounced dead."

41

About three hours later following an uneventful northbound drive through the Alps and East-Central Switzerland we came to the small city of Vaduz, which with about 5000 inhabitants still made it capital of the tiny principality of Lichtenstein, tucked away in a mountain valley between the Swiss canton of St. Galen on the south and west and Austria on the east and north. It was still early for lunch, and I said let's go visit one of the law firms in town. I understand there are more lawyers here than people. But Rona opined,

"Hey, I know what you want to find, Michael, but you're kidding yourself. This town has made its name out of hiding wealthy people's money. The parent company of BC Development, Ltd., registered here in Lichtenstein, is almost certainly a holding company with no more than a mailbox in Vaduz. Or maybe that holding company in turn is held by a trust held in a bank for the real owner, and protected by the strict bank secrecy laws of Lichtenstein, which are even more impregnable than Switzerland's. In any event you'll never discover the identity of the real person behind BC Development, Ltd."

" I'm sure you're right, Rona. But although we both know Seth Frankenheim is the ultimate bad guy in our story, we must find some way to prove his connection to the murders in Jerusalem and Cyprus with real, hard evidence. Otherwise we'd never be able to get the Swiss authorities do anything to Frankenheim. And in that case we won't be able to legally recover the stolen ossuary from Switzerland. So I thought it was worth a try before we turn to more efficient, covert self help methods, that the Swiss would certainly raise hell about if they ever found out."

At the end of a long, tedious day Rona was of course proven correct. Though we went to several of the largest law firms, banks and the other establishments specializing in consulting, management and insurance in town we could find nothing about the identity of the real person or persons behind BC Development, Ltd. It was easy to find advice in this place about how to hide money and identity, but it was absolutely impossible to find information on the seekers and beholders of advice. No wonder. This was the reason the midget principality became a financial giant and the third richest country in the world.

We drove out of the little town, found a hotel set inside a park overlooking Vaduz and its medieval castle and settled into a comfortable guestroom open into a balcony. I walked out to the balcony while Rona flicked the TV set open. I was standing there staring absently at the vista of the Rhine valley, the vineyards and the Alps turning rose, purple and red in light of the setting sun, and pondering the next move when Rona shouted come here, Michael. Come quick. I rushed to the room. She was indicating the TV screen, featuring Seth Frankenheim enigmatically fixing a pair of blue eyes down his narrow, chiseled nose at the camera.

42

The camera zoomed out, showing Frankenheim standing beside a fiftyish woman, a reporter, in front of the closed door of an Eighteenth century chateau. The woman gestured around them, the camera zoomed out again, showing acres of beautifully landscaped gardens on the shore of a lake. She asked in French,

"Are you happy to live here, Mr. Frankenheim? I realize you have been used to living in luxury, in a splendid Palace hotel in Paris, the City of Lights. When I interviewed you there two years ago I found the beauty of that particular refined hotel captivating, with its exceptional location and grandeur. It truly evokes the alluring history of Paris. You had a luxury apartment there with a striking view of the Place de la Concorde , the inner courtyards of the Louvre and the gardens of the Tuilleries. You told me you've selected that hotel over some of France's most famous palatial chateaux because you prefer to overlook the greatest museum in the world than abide in verdant settings far from urban crowds. What caused you to change your mind and move to this chateau in a little village by the lake of Geneva?"

"I'm still quite content here. I don't have the Louvre, but I can quietly enjoy my private collections, in total privacy as I prefer."

"Yes. I read a few more articles about you in preparation for today's interview. What I found truly fascinating was the quest for archeological artifacts. You seem to have a dual mind; one of a businessman and one of a collector. True?"

"Yes. That is the exact crossover I fall into quite happily in all of my endeavors, be they in business or just daily living. I seem to be inspired in both directions you mention: archeology and its business use. I acquired some fascinating antiquities recently that I can admire whenever I want, far from the maddening crowds of a museum."

"I'd like to show our viewers the inside of the chateau now, Mr. Frankenheim."

"By all means, come in. It has thirty rooms."

I moved quickly to the VCR inside the TV desk below the screen and pushed the record button, but it said empty, get cassette. I took five steps back and sat down on the bed next to Rona on her wheelchair. At that point the camera took a slow round shot inside the large entrance hall of the chateau. I noticed a security device blinking next to a metal door. The reporter pointed at that door and asked where that elevator leads to. Frankenheim said to my private collection. As you see. It's real, real private. The reporter said let's go see the upper floor now, and they both began climbing a spiral stairway. I took the phone book from the night table beside the bed. Rona said who do you want to call, Michael. I said a friend from the squadron who I used to fly with back in the air force. His name is Kaplan, but now he lives in Zurich and goes by name of Bruce Kaplan. He's become a fabulously rich man. About as big a wheel in Switzerland as Frankenheim obviously is. By that time the reporter was thanking the latter for taking the time to share the lifestyle of the rich and famous with common folks. He said no problem, I waste a lot of my time in other places, like going every night to play the roulette at the Divonne casino. She said thank you again all the same and the TV started another program. I walked back to the TV table, took the TV programming brochure and found that the same interview was going to air again later in that evening, went down to the hotel's office and asked for a recording cassette, but they said we don't have new cassettes and can't give you a recorded one. I said how much does a new cassette cost, they said 15 francs, I said I'll give you 25 for a recorded cassette, they said no. I said 100 francs and got it. Returned to the room and later recorded the second broadcast of the interview in its entirety. Then I called Bruce Kaplan and fixed a meeting with him on the next day, a Sunday, 3;30 P.M. at a Zurich café on Bahnhofstrasse.

43

The Confiserie Sprungli at Paradplatz and Bahnhoffstrasse in Zurich is known as a shrine to chocolate, purveyor of regular to exotic chocolate confections. By the time Rona and I got there the ground floor shop was packed with customers eyeing the mouth- watering variety of sweets exhibited there. We went over to an elevator inside the shop and took it to the café located on the first floor. Zurich's chocolatiers also baked the best pastries in town, which is certainly why so many locals crowded into this noisy, oblong room with large brass chandeliers overhanging round wood and glass coffee tables. Most patrons were munching on pastel colored mini "burgers" that looked overly sweet to me. Kaplan was sitting by one of the tables overlooking the pedestrians on Bahnhoffstrasse. He waved gaily to us, we came over and sat by the table next to him, ordered champagne truffles with coffees after the introductions and began tasting them. He asked what brings me to Zurich and I considered the noisy place safe enough for a preliminary discussion of the matter in Hebrew and confided,

"We're treasure hunting for an ancient relic that was smuggled out of Israel, Bruce. But we won't be able to recover it using official channels."

"Sounds interesting. Why don't we finish our snacks and then you two follow me to my house. I drive a vintage red Rolls Royce and it wouldn't be pushed very fast even if I wanted to, so you don't risk losing me.

It's about two kilometers along the lake turning left at the end of Bahnhoffstrasse, and then left again and a short distance up a hill."

At Kaplan's home we used a computer to enlarge the view of the elevator inside Frankenheim's chateau that I had copied on the VCR cassette. A rectangular metal device with a glass surface lay on a decorative tall stand next to the elevator.

"Platen," said Rona. "You place your finger on it, light shines upon the parts of the fingertip touching the glass and the formed image is captured."

"Of course, baby. It's an optical fingerprint image capture system, involving a light source that is refracted through a prism. Seth protects the access to this elevator with the latest biometrics technology, and we both know what that elevator leads to."

"I will do everything to help you retrieve the object from him and bring it back to Israel," said Kaplan. "What do you need, Michael?"

"Start with providing us both new identity documents, and end with making sure to have your private Astra bizjet ready for me on the tarmac at Cointrin airport in Geneva on short notice. I hope it's not as glitzy as your car."

"It's fashion designed, Michael. It usually requires two pilots, but it'd still fly you to Israel non stop if you haven't lost your touch. It needs a slow, sensitive hand, and the stick will fully and eagerly respond with timely precision."

"Don't you worry, Bruce," pronounced Rona, smiling broadly. "He's getting better all the time."

44

At the breakfast table on the following day I asked Kaplan for the location of a chemical supplies store in Zurich. He gave me an address in the industrial part of the city. Then asked what I want to buy there. SPR, I said. And what's that? Small Particle Reagent, said Rona. That's another name for Molybendum Disulfide, which is difficult to say. SPR is a physical development technique where small black particles adhere to the fatty substances left in fingerprint residue. Gotcha, said Kaplan. Got to run, folks. Here are two guns for you. Here's a duplicate set of my keys for the Astra . Here's an address in Luzern where you can get Swiss IDs. Tell the operator there Kaplan sent you. Here's my private cell phone number. Return your SUV to Avis in Zurich and then call me. Bye.

"Nice guy," said Rona as Kaplan left the house.

"Not very small, either. But it's too late to swap. He's taken, and so are you."

She placed down the warmed brioche we brought from Sprungli's and caressed my cheek,

"I'm afraid I'm hooked already on a guy who's not exactly my idea of physical masculine perfection."

"I like that in you. Come to think of it, maybe I should have asked Bruce to take the five penny tour of Frankenheim's chateau with me. Maybe I'd have a hard time carrying that ossuary around by myself, once I get to it."

"Don't worry. That women's hairdresser already must have given you a nod 2000 years ago."

"You mean Magdala Nashia? What's she got to do with it? You're mixing apples with oranges."

"Cucumbers with pumpkins, is what she would probably have said."

"You lost me. What the heck are you talking about, Rona?"

"The Talmud reflects one sexual idiom from the period, and one only- 'he with his large cucumber and she with her small pumpkins.' They didn't even have apples or oranges in the Holy Land at that time."

"Amusing. And what does this have to do with my hauling difficulties re that bone box?"

"It appears that Magdala Nashia also had a preference for brain over size."

"As they say, a good perfume comes in a small bottle. You mean the resident of the subject bone box was a compact guy, like me?"

"Bring me the Bible from the bookshelf there, and I'll show you."

"Yes, Master Argov." I brought the book and sat by her again.

"Here it is, Michael, John 20:15 'She said to him, sir if you have taken him away, tell me where you've laid him, and I will take him away.' If Mary Magdalene could by herself carry the body of Jesus of Nazareth, you should be able to carry the limestone box that probably held his skeletal remains. "

45

I opened one or two of the kitchen drawers, found and took a plastic sealing bag used to preserve food. Then we left the house to the chemicals supply store, where I bought an SPR fingerprint hand spray. Next we drove to the Avis rental car location in central Zurich, a few streets west of Bahnhoffstrasse, where we returned the SUV. We stepped out of the Avis office and I called Kaplan. He said go to the Jelmoli department store a few blocks away, just off Bahnhoffstrasse. Do some shopping there for half an hour and then sit in the café on the second floor. One of my employees will come, bring you keys for another vehicle, a white van, that you will use from now on. The van will be parked at the Jelmoli public garage. After you finish the business in Luzern drive directly to Geneva. When you get there go to the Parc des Eaux–Vives hotel. I've made reservations for you. We complied and an hour later I was driving a white van on the way to Luzern.

We came to Luzern city at the western end of the Lake of Luzern in less than an hour, crossed a long modern bridge at the edge of the lake to the south side of the river Reuss, took a right and drove along the left bank past two ancient wooden bridges for pedestrians until we came to another concrete bridge, turned right and crossed the river again, turned right again and drove inside an octagonal medieval tower , part of the old city wall, came to a small square and pulled the white van to park diagonally by one of the meters along the curb.

After I prepared the wheelchair and settled Rona in it, we strolled into the cobbled winding streets of the old city. In about five minutes we came to a Kornmarkt square, featuring the town hall and a beautifully painted Pfistern Guildhall.

The address Kaplan gave us turned out to be a small watch repair shop on a narrow street extending from this square. We opened the glass door and stepped inside. A short bespectacled middle aged man greeted us in German. I told him in English Mr. Kaplan sent us, and he invited me to follow him into a small artisan's studio located behind the counter, while Rona remained in the shop. I then explained to him what we needed. He said get your companion here, I need to make passport photos of both of you. After we took these photos he said return at 2:30 P.M. I looked at my watch and it was noon. We exited the store to the freezing but sunny, picturesque old town.

Strolling down a diminutive alley we came to the right bank of the river, took a left along the arcaded Rathausquai, and arrived at a small open area flanked by a St. Peter's Chapel on the left, and a long, wooden bridge across the river to the right. A panel described this as Chapel Bridge, constructed in the early part of the Fourteenth century. Rona drove her wheelchair onto it, and I followed. She proceeded on the creaking wooden beams, her head uplifted to the paintings decorating the ceiling, illustrating scenes of Swiss and local history. When she arrived at the southern end of the bridge she took a right onto the left bank of the river, I followed in a faster pace to join her and walked by her

side. We proceeded   several hundred meters along the
riverbank until we came to another ancient wooden
bridge, called the Spreuer Bridge. This one was
constructed in the early Seventeenth century. It was
shorter than the Chapel Bridge, but contained more
paintings, all representing the "Dance of Death." I
mused how that theme was appropriate to our presence
in the place, all things considered, but didn't share this
remarkable impression with Rona. She was clearly
enjoying the scenery tremendously.

The Spreuer Bridge ended just at the edge of the
small square where we had previously parked our van. I
went over to the central meter machine and bought a
continuance for two hours. Rona said time for lunch,
indicating a small restaurant on the east side of the
square. We entered the restaurant and had a delightful
lunch by a long glass window, open to the riverbank
below us. An hour or so later we returned to the little
watch repair shop. Picked up two drivers' licenses issued
by the Canton of Geneva, in the form of blue booklets
bearing French sounding names on the left side and our
photos on the right side, respectively. Also picked up
two Swiss identity cards bearing the same names under
the same photographs. Paid the operator in cash,
returned to our van, hit the motorway and drove
through the winter scenery of a snow bordered asphalt
road   along a procession of lakes and white capped
mountains toward Interlaken, Bern, Friburg, Vevey,
Lausanne and Geneva in about four hours.

When we came to Geneva we checked into the
hotel of Parc des Eaux Vives, a historical renovated

building on top of a large verdant park overlooking lake Geneva. One of the seven guestrooms of the hotel was already reserved under our new Swiss names, everything prepaid. We presented our Swiss identity cards and retired to the room.

Rona called Tal Walden and asked him to meet her at 9:30 on the next evening at the entrance to the Divonne casino. Then we both dressed up, took a mirrored elevator to the polished brasserie style restaurant on the ground floor and had a sumptuous dinner at a table set elegantly by a window opening to a panoramic view of the lake, its northwest shore, a myriad of impressive buildings housing international organizations perched in the hills behind it, including the huge complex of the former League of Nations, and the Jura Mountains farther to the northwest framing the scene.

46

On the next evening at 9:05 I drove Rona from the Parc des Aux Vives through the center of Geneva, past the Mont Blanc bridge to the right on Quai Wilson, then along the motorway to Lausanne, took the Coppet exit about twenty minutes later, turned left into the westbound road to Divonne les Bains just across the French border and eight minutes later parked near the casino building. There I settled Rona into her wheelchair, kissed her, said good luck baby, watched her gracefully maneuvering the wheelchair into the casino's reception hall, drove back to the hotel and sat on a sofa in the lobby overlooking the entrance.

She made her entry to the lobby around midnight, smiling triumphantly and waiving her handbag. I walked over in stride to her and kissed her on the mouth. Three minutes later we were back in our grand guestroom.

She opened the handbag and brought out the plastic sealing bag, proudly indicating a crystalline wine glass inside it. I said tell me. She said I saw Frankenheim sitting by a roulette table, punched "record" on this little Sony that I always carry in my handbag. The rest is all here. She put a small mini cassette recorder on the elegant desk facing the bed and pressed the play button. It all came out nice and clear.

Rona: "Mind if I join the table next to you, Mr. Frankenheim?"

Frankenheim: "I'd love that, Ms. Argov. I adore the close proximity of exquisite beauty."

Rona: "I thought so. You seem to have a terminal attraction to relics."

Frenkenheim: "But you're no relic, Ms. Argov. In fact, seated women exude the essence of feminine enchantment. That's why the most outstanding paintings of beautiful women in art's history have been taken in that position."

Humming of the crowd around the tables, sound of the wheel turning, the ball bouncing, croupier stating "rien ne va plus," then declaring "cinq treize vingt quatre, rouge; five-thirteen-twenty four. You won, Mr. Frankenheim."

Rona: " Lucky, too. Along comes the waitress, shall we drink to that? Here, take this whiskey, sir."

Frankenheim: "I'll drink it for you. But I actually prefer red wine. Wait, let me put my chips on the table, before that croupier closes this round. He has already stated 'faites vos jeux'."

Rona: "Five-thirteen-twenty four again. Are you superstitious, Mr. Frankenheim?"

Frankenheim: "Eccentric, rather."

Rona : "Here comes the waitress again. Take this glass of red wine, since you prefer that. I won't force you to drink vulgar whiskey, that you don't like. Give me that whiskey glass and I'll put it aside for you."

Frankenheim : "Well, why bother yourself with disposing that. I'll just hand the whiskey back to the waitress. Now I'll drink my red wine, all for you."

Usual casino humdrum again. The croupier announcing "twenty five-one- eighteen."Rona saying "goodbye Mr. Frankenheim. Your luck has left you and so must I." Tape clicking off. I exclaimed,

"Great. And then how did you get the wine glass?"

"Simple, my love. He put the empty glass on the table beside him, picked a second glass from another circulating waitress and turned his attention to the croupier. At which time I just picked the empty glass from the table and hid it beneath the shawl I had over my legs. Then I bid farewell to Frankenheim and made my departure from the roulette. Rolled to the ladies room, wiped the inside of the glass, inserted it carefully into the plastic sealing bag and put it back into my handbag. Next I joined Tal Walden at the blackjack table. After he lost all his money there we left the casino, he drove me back, and here I am."

"You're my one and only wonder woman. In which hand did Frankenheim hold the wine glass, baby?"

"His right hand."

I took the plastic bag from her, went over to my suitcase, took out the SPR aerosol, sprayed the inside of the bag containing the wine glass well with the chemical, closed the bag air tight, placed the sealed plastic on the lower shelf of the mahogany TV desk facing the bed, jumped on the same and said come on baby, this is certainly a good pretext for celebration.

When we relaxed from sexual ecstasy about an hour later I rolled off the bed, took the plastic bag and opened it carefully. The wine glass bore a neat ridge arrangement in black color, a pattern unique to Seth Frankenheim. I took out one of the latex gloves, slipped it on my right hand, placed my thumb slowly over the print and lifted it carefully from the surface. I examined the glove and saw that the print was neatly arranged on the thumb, sighed in relief and returned contentedly to bed.

47

Early in the morning on the next day I ran the cassette of Frankenheim's interview on the VCR in our hotel room. Paused the picture at the very beginning and approached the screen to examine the door before which Frankneheim was standing. It had a cylindrical knob lock. I pushed the play button again until the point where Frankenheim and his interviewer step inside the house and the camera shoots a slow 360 of that. I paused the tape where it showed the walls beside the door. No burglar alarm control mechanism there. Rewound the tape to the view of the landscaped yard, rolling to the beach. No dogs to be seen there. Seth doesn't believe in alarms, mechanical or biological. Knows what I know that dingers don't really keep serious burglars out of a house. Lots of trees and bushes though, constituting a live fence along the property line. Probably has a security gate at the entrance, too. I asked Rona to call Walden for the address of the chateau. She said I already asked him that yesterday, darling. It's in Versoix, at the end of a cul de sac aptly named "Chemin de la Greve."

Twenty some minutes later we were sitting in the van driving to Versoix. When we got there we turned right into the cul de sac, which means "strand road" in French. The imposing chateau blocked the end of the road. A wide sliding metal grille was towering before a circular driveway. The black Mercedes I stuffed in Milan was parked there along a sleek gold colored Porche. I stopped the van and cut the engine off, rolled down the windows to get a better sense of the place. Some bird on the tree closest to us began singing three short low pitched notes bup, bup, bup, then louder ee-oh-lay, finally a rapid ventriloquial phrase. Then many birds joined in with their own repertoires. Isn't that lovely marveled Rona. Sure, baby, I agreed. But we got to go prepare our own grand entrance to this leafy place. I restarted the engine and drove back toward Geneva on the surface road along the lake. After a few hundred meters I saw a sideway leading to the shore, and a sign indicating "Centre Nautique Moby-Dick." I took a left, drove down that sideway less than twenty meters to the beach front and stopped the van right by the water. There was a landing and a large sign over it, offering motor boats, row boats and pedal boats for rent, by the hour or on a daily rate. Rona said how about lunch now, Michael? I started the engine, returned to the surface road toward Geneva, drove a few hundred meters until I saw a sign indicating a restaurant du Creux de Genthod, turned left into another short sideway and parked the van closest to the lake.

It was the perfect spot to go on that bright, sunny winter day. We sat in an outdoor terrace overlooking the lake with the Mont Blanc Massif in the background. They had a menu, but I saw pretty much everyone around us went for the filets de perches, a local specialty. We ordered the same, and within minutes a large plate of filets of perch was served to us in a butter sauce with Pommes Frites. The meal paired nicely with a bottle of Rose d'Anjou. Rona produced a small camera from her bag and clicked it at the beautiful surrounding, took a deep breath and offered,

"I'm going to go there tonight with you, Michael. You know that."

"No way, girl. This is a man's job."

"Spare me the chauvinist session. I'm going with you. You said yourself you'd need some help."

"I was talking about big Bruce Kaplan. Not a...girl."

"You meant to say a handicapped female, right? At least let me go in the boat with you. That's certainly going to raise much less suspicion than a solo macho renting a motorboat on a winter evening."

"Okay, baby. You're right as always. What can I say. But if you do come along, we'd better drive to the central train station in Geneva, rent two cell phones, so as to communicate better from this point on."

"Will do, soon as we sample the desserts here. From the train station we'll return to that huge park housing our little historical hotel. Take a nap, change to burglars' garb complete with Kaplan's guns in our coat pockets and hit into Frankenheim's castle, after which we'll return the particular piece of holy land history he lifted to the only nation and country where   it properly belongs."

We topped our lunch with a platter of local cheeses then left to do the job.

48

And so it was that in the late afternoon of the same sunny winter day we returned to the small landing on the lakefront at Versoix, named after a perennial huge white whale, and rented a small motor boat there. The operator of the place asked for how long we want it. I said we'll pay upfront for 24 hours, adding I guess I'd have to look hard for Moby- Dick among the diminutive filets of perche swimming in this tub. He didn't smile. Must be a typical French-Swiss fellow, I thought. Humor doesn't even exist in this culture, centered rather on the notion of ridicule.

But he did help me settle Rona into the boat and handed me her folded wheelchair after I jumped in. I said thanks, started the engine, steered about twenty meters into the lake, and then turned to the right, in opposite direction to Frankenheim's chateau. We came close to the shore, nearest to the Jet d'Eaux, the most famous landmark of Geneva, used as a safety valve for a power generator, which was throwing waters of the lake up about thirty meters in the clear, quickly darkening sky. We sat in the boat at the same area admiring the scenery for several hours. When complete darkness fell all around us I turned the wheel 180 degrees and followed the western coastline northbound. We passed the boat rental place where there was nobody, proceeded a few hundred meters to the north, and recognized the chateau perched on its strand. I slowed the engine to the lowest rpm, turned the wheel perpendicular to the large building, and beached the boat, bow on the pebble and stern in the water. Moved Rona back by the wheel within reach of the engine starter, kissed her on her full lips and stepped ashore. A lonely owl hooted a short alarm, but nobody was around to heed this sentinel of the night.

I moved silently along a path among some chestnut trees to the front of the chateau, took my wallet out of my black coat's breast pocket and selected a plastic credit card from it. Next I slid the card slowly into the lock mechanism and wiggled it between the door and the jamb. Then I pulled it gradually toward me, turning the handle and pushing it inside at the same time. With a slight creak the door opened away from the jamb toward the inside of the house. I pushed it a little more, just enough to be able to peep inside. Reached for my coat's pocket, took a large, heavy metal flashlight, turned it on and moved it about the large entrance hall. Nobody there. I pushed the door some more and stepped inside. All quiet on that front. Closed the door behind me in total silence, pointed the flashlight to the elevator, and walked slowly to the biometric fingerprint security device. Standing next to it I stripped the black leather glove I was wearing on my right hand, leaving its match on my left hand. Took out the right latex glove from my pocket and slipped it on my right hand. So far so good.

I placed my right hand thumb on the glass plate surface of the fingerprint reader and pulled the door of the elevator. It opened smoothly and silently.

I stepped into the elevator, closed   it's door carefully, pointed the flashlight to the control panel and pushed the single button there. The elevator responded with modern efficiency and brought me to a lower floor. Pushed the door open and I was standing at one end of a short, narrow corridor, blocked by a vault door at the other end. I walked over to the bank style door and examined it under my flashlight. It had a bolt protected by a three-tumbler key change combination lock.

I placed my left hand on the combination lock and turned it clockwise in sequence five-thirteen-twenty four. Pulled on the handle and the door turned with micron-range precision on its roller-thrust bearing hinges. I put my left hand inside the breast pocket of my coat, pulled out my gun, stepped into the stale opening and turned the flashlight around with my right hand.

It was a whitewashed bunker-like space about the size of an average bedroom. There was nothing in it but one small wooden crate lying on the floor at the far left corner. I moved over to it. The lid was open and I pointed the flashlight inside the crate. At that precise moment someone shined another flashlight on the bare concrete wall just above my head, and a familiar voice announced,

"Welcome Inspector Inbar. I was waiting for you."

I pivoted to face him, pointed the gun in my left hand to the gun he was holding in his right hand and pronounced,

"Ain't no skin off my nose, Frankenheim. I was expecting you too."

49

"For a fall guy, turns out I was correct that you'd still be capable of following my clues into this final resting place, Inspector."

"You can whistle past the graveyard, chump. My superiors may have for some time underestimated my mental capacity to track the treasure because of my impairment following a personal tragedy. But now I'm going to take it with me."

"Over my dead body, Inbar. It stays here until I eventually tire of admiring it. Go have a look of it. I won't shoot you while you're at it."

"You seemed quite eager to dispose of me previously, what with that   ape man throwing me over the ridge at the Mont Blanc, trying to bump my SUV on the Autostrada to Milan and being generally sort of unfriendly."

"You mean Kalman? He's usually an efficient terminator, but he couldn't promptly dispose of you, so I thought I'd best get you into this trap. Anyway he's not here right now. Go ahead, examine the ossuary. I didn't bring you all the way here just to kill you without having you see it first."

I shined the flashlight again on the limestone inside the wooden crate, informing,

"I can't read the inscription from this position. But it is clearly preceded by a large cross mark, which is shifted sideways with the lateral arm longer than the horizontal arm. I know already that this is the exact form of the Hebrew letter Taw, in ancient script, and that it signified the Messiah in Jewish tradition going back to at least the second century BC. I know already also that the Greek letter equivalent to the Hebrew Taw is Tau, which has also acquired spiritual symbolical meaning in the Roman-Hellenistic world. What else is new, Frankenheim?"

"Another Greek letter, the Chi, was also recognized as an equivalent of the Taw. The Chi is written in the same way as this sign on the ossuary, similar to the Latin X. And Chi is the first letter of the Greek word Christos, Christ. This word in turn is the usual translation of the Hebrew word 'annointed', or 'Messiah'."

"Messiah or not, the relic of this Jew belongs among his proper nation and in his proper country, which is called Israel nowadays. I'll return it presently to Jerusalem, unless you insist on that 'over my dead body' bravado, in which case   I'll have to accommodate you. Seth you up for hell, so to speak."

"Why don't you first consider my reasons for bringing it here, Inbar. Originally I didn't want to take it out of Israel, but I was left with no other choice."

"You mean you'd have put it in a private museum that BC Development, Ltd would have constructed at the original spot of the burial cave in Dov Gruner street, East Talpiot? Not a bad idea, and I have good reason to believe that the Israel Lands Administration would have permitted the acquisition of the property for the construction of such a museum after rezoning by the proper Jerusalem city real estate commission."

"We were about to do just that when you foiled our plan, Inspector. It would have become a high place for Christian tourism, as predicted curiously even in your Talmud. A passage in Berachot 30a equates 'Talpiot' mystically to a place of the highest worship, explaining that it denotes :"the elevation [tel] towards which all mouths (piyyoth) turn'."

"I wouldn't have interfered in that plan if you hadn't behaved real nasty about procuring the ossuaries for the museum. That had incited my interest in this affair. Burglary first, followed by a murder-burglary, then a murder in Cyprus of that apartment building resident. Why the excessive violence?"

"Moshe Cohen discovered the full value of his apartment to us, and wanted too much money to sell it and keep quiet. The museum guard stood in our way, and had to go. Since we were going to construct a museum at the site of the burial cave, we needed the ossuaries originally found in that cave for exhibition at that museum. The very bones for the visitors to grind on, so to speak. But your Knesset had passed a law in Israel in or about 1978, which makes all antiquities found in Israel property of the State."

"So you couldn't purchase the ossuaries from the Israel Antiquities Authority. But you could probably lease them for a long term, say ninety-nine years. This way you could still legally exhibit them in your museum."

"That's how we intended to solve the problem originally, but we were given to understand your government would not under any circumstances agree to be perceived as having anything to do with a grand exposure of these particular ossuaries, complete with media hype and all other gimmicks of marketing hoopla."

"And you thought that once you got the ossuaries by means of an 'acceptable' level of violence, such as a little burglary, they would let you go? Why would they want to do that?"

"I told you once, Inspector, that I was about to make your country a lot of money by substantially increasing tourism to it. Christian oriented tourism. The attraction of Christ is enormous, even with a patently fake relic, as you've seen in Turin. That shroud fabricated in France in the Fourteenth century brings millions of tourists annually to northern Italy, thus not only filling the coffers of the owners of the museum exhibiting it, but enriching mostly the government and population of Italy. Imagine how much more this authentic relic of Christ could have done for the benefit of your country and people."

"Very good. I'll return it to Israel and it will be exhibited shortly in a public museum. The Israel Museum does come to mind. But according to you, the government would do everything it can to prevent being identified with promotion and exhibition of this particular archeological item, let alone officially recognizing its magnitude. So as to avoid stepping on the toes of some Christian sects, I presume?"

"Exactly. Only by allowing me to exhibit it in my private museum, while being unable to prove we stole it from under its nose, could your government conceivably have the cake and eat it, too. Why did you think the police high echelons entrusted this very investigation to an inspector impaired by major depression?"

"The suspicion had occurred to me that Dayan didn't really want me to find hard evidence of your involvement in murders, connected to the subject ossuaries, sufficient to prove it beyond reasonable doubt. However, I'm sure you wouldn't have been able to actually display these ossuaries in the museum, if they were known to be stolen, let alone cause for murder. So your plan was hanging on a very slender thread. Anyway now that you've smuggled the jewel in the crown out of Israel, Dayan honestly wants it back, and realizes that after all I'm still the best man he has for this mission."

"You've left me no alternative. Once you got the evidence of David Barnes's involvement in crimes, the whole scheme crumbled. So I used my back up plan and got this ossuary here. You have no idea how your description of it as jewel in the crown hits precisely on the nails of the matter."

"As royal as it may be, I'll take it now. Move aside if you care to stay in freedom and good health. Hasta la vista."

"Not so quick. I'll shoot you if you even touch it. I told your striking companion that I'll kill for possession of exquisite relics."

"My same companion read to me just the other day a passage from the New Testament, where it says 'take heed, and beware of all covetousness; for a man's life does not consist of the abundance of his possessions.' But you obviously disagree, at least with that part. You leave her out of the equation, Frankenheim, or you'd find my attraction to her fatal to yourself."

"I don't blame you. She's the kind of woman that men would eagerly die for. Her pictures don't do her justice. Stunning. So, why don't we split these marvelous possessions, you take the beauty and I take the king. I realize you're a dedicated person, so I won't do the silly thing and offer you money. Now go in peace."

I dropped the gun from my left hand while throwing the heavy flashlight at the same time with my right straight at Frankenheim's puzzled face, his eyes detracted to the floor. He dropped his gun from his right hand and his flashlight from his left hand, held his forehead with both, fell forward with a heavy thud and disappeared in the ensuing total darkness. I bent down to the spot where I dropped my gun, felt it with my fingers, lifted it and held it in Frankenheim's direction. But he was dead calm now.

50

I extended my arms forward and walked straight, in slow, hesitant steps toward the spot where I'd last seen Frankenheim standing. My mind must have been somehow compressing the distance to him however because I thought I still had a few steps more to go when I stumbled on his body, lost some balance but managed to remain standing. I then bent to the ground around me, fumbled for several minutes and finally found a flashlight, turned it on and pointed it to Frankenheim.

He was lying face down on the floor, certainly in no condition to give me any problems for at least several days to come. I touched his temple and realized he was alive. Searched his pockets and found two keys on a fancy Mercedes chain, held it, lifted his gun from the floor and placed both items into my coat's pocket. At that moment a giant figure in red pajamas swooshed by me, causing the flashlight to fall from my hand. Here comes Kalman, I thought. Probably missing the zoo. He must have been holding his own flashlight, because at that time the only object I could see there was the small wooden crate, shining in the center of a round spotlight. But then Kalman must have picked the crate up. Because it had disappeared and the spotlight was rounded now on the far side of the whitewashed wall to my left. That same part of the wall then itself disappeared. I felt fresh air blowing on my face, fired a shot in the dark, saw light in a short tunnel extending to the moonlit shrubs outside and ran into it after Kalman. I fired another shot in his general direction, then emerged into the backyard. I heard a shot and ducked to the ground, watching Kalman's silhouette rounding the corner of the chateau. Someone fired two more shots in rapid succession. I stood up, ran quickly along the wall of the chateau, reached the corner, saw Kalman opening the driver door of the Porche and pushing the wooden crate inside, then jumping in. I began moving after him. Before I made two steps he had started the engine of the Porche and drove it fast toward the sliding gate. It opened and he zoomed the sports car into the small street.

I ran over to the black Mercedes, fumbled for the keys, started the engine and drove slowly toward the gate. It opened again, I revved the engine and speeded the big car after the Porche. Then I called Rona on the cell phone. I said how are you baby she said fine, what's cooking? I said I'm following the big bad guy who has the treasure, and now I don't know if I should continue after him or return to you. She said get him first and then come back to me. Like a bad check, I know you'll always return. And what happened to the smaller bad guy? I said he won't be seen at any fashionable hangout for the rest of this winter. She said I'd still better get out of here. I'll start the engine of the boat, shift the gear into reverse and power off the pebble beach into the lake. Then I'll steer the boat to the Moby Dick landing where our white van is parked and wait for your return there. Don't be scared off darling, you know they insist that size doesn't really matter. I wondered whether she was alluding to Kalman or to the whale, but said nothing more about that and kept my weary eyes on the Porche ahead.

At that point the Porche was slowing down for the passage through the Swiss-French border. It stopped for a French border official, who came over to it and had the usual short exchange with Kalman. I could hear it as I was stopped one meter behind the Porche. The Frenchman then waived Kalman through and uttered the buzzwords to me. No I don't have anything to declare I said. At least I wasn't lying like Kalman, who by that time was proceeding to the south on the practically empty motorway. I followed him right after the Frenchman waived me through, but when the Porche came out of the latter's sight Kalman obviously floored the accelerator. I had to do the same and within seconds we were racing ahead at speeds of over 220 km/h, slowing sometimes only to overtake saner drivers.

A few more minutes passed and then I saw the Porche turning into an off-- ramp indicating Annecy, centre ville. I followed onto the same off-- ramp, my tires screeching, just in time to see the Porche speed along a scenic canal lit with Parisian style lamps on black lampposts, through a narrow pedestrian passage between ancient apartment buildings, and disappear. I realized the passage was too narrow for the Mercedes. Therefore I stopped it by the canal and ran into the passage. It led into a small courtyard, featuring the same lighting, from which forked two other barely lit narrow passages. I chose the passage to the right, ran through it, found nothing, returned to the courtyard and ran into the other passage. A few steps into it I saw the Porche parked by another canal, on a road too narrow even for this little sports car to move along. I took my gun out and proceeded carefully toward the car. Reached the end of the passage and peeped slowly around the opening. Nothing there. He couldn't be hiding on the inner wall of the canal. Could he? I walked carefully to that canal. At that point I had a glimpse of red pajamas jumping from behind the Porche. Kalman kicked me in the groin. I fell to the ground holding on to that possession. Kalman stooped to pick my gun from the cobbled pavement muttering prepare to die, Inbar. I rolled swiftly on the ground, put my hand into my coat pocket and fired one shot through the woolen material with Frankenheim's gun, straight into Kalman's big frame. He stood erect, clutched his chest with his huge paws, stumbled four steps backward and fell head first into the muddy water of the canal below. I went over to my gun and picked it up, then walked to the left side of the Porche, opened the unlocked driver door, found the keys in the ignition, started the engine and idled the car slowly from the scene of the battle. It was 1:01 A.M. according to the Porche's display screen, therefore I wasn't surprised that nobody seemed to be watching me depart with the little wooden crate nestled in the passenger seat. Twenty- five minutes later I stopped the Porche back at the parking area of the Moby Dick landing, shifted the automatic gear to park, turned off the engine and exited the car.

51

Rona was sitting alone in the boat, bow beached on the pebble by the landing. She waved to me. I ran over to her, jumped to the boat and hugged her. She was shivering and blurted,

"Kiss me Michael. I worried for you so."

"I didn't worry enough for you, baby. What were these shots I heard as I rushed through the backyard after Kalman?"

"About an hour and a half after you entered the chateau I heard a shot, then I saw that big man in red pajamas, Kalman I guess, darting out of a secret passage opening to the backyard, carrying a crate like a toy between his arms. Then I heard another shot. I understood it must be you chasing after Kalman. Seconds later another man emerged from a small wood cabin among the trees to the right of the chateau, ran along the façade, then stood at the corner of the building and fired a shot in the direction of the secret passage opening. He must have been a guard. I took out the gun Kaplan gave me and fired two shots into the chateau's masonry, just above his head. At that point I saw you proceeding along the wall toward the front of the chateau. I aimed at the guard intending a direct hit if needed to prevent him from shooting you in the back. The guard didn't shoot. Instead he turned around, saw me aiming my gun at him, ducked and jumped to the door that you'd unlocked earlier, turned the handle, pushed the door open, leaped inside and closed it again behind him. I kept my gun aimed at the door for about two minutes more, he didn't come out. Then you called me on the cell phone about chasing Kalman and the bone box. I guess you have it now inside that fancy sports car. And where's the big bad guy?"

I took a long time kissing her and then mumbled,

"I'm afraid at this time Kalman is floating in a canal at Annecy, or maybe he's already in the lake that feeds these canals. Hope he prefers goldfish over the golden Porche."

On that note I lifted Rona on my arms, stepped out of the boat, carried her to the white van, settled her in the passenger seat, returned to the boat, tied it to the landing and brought out the wheelchair to the van. Then I took the wooden crate out of the Porche, placed it also inside the van, said I'll be back in ten minutes, Rona, and drove the Porche to Chemin de la Greve.

The chateau's gate was closed. I parked the Porche on the street closest to the gate, put the keys inside the console between the bucket seats, stepped out of the car and quietly closed the driver's door, then took off running on the asphalt surface road toward Geneva, my feet thumping a regular rhythm mingling with the usual sounds of the night. I ran this way on the empty road for about five minutes until I reached the lakeside landing, opened the driver door of the van and settled on the seat next to Rona, breathing heavily. I said let's go back baby, started the engine and drove to the Parc des Aux Vives on the opposite side of the lake. There I parked the van, emptied the contents of my coat's pockets, placed them on Rona's lap, stepped out of the van and looked around me. Nobody. Took off my long black coat, opened the backdoor of the van and covered the wooden crate with it. Then I brought out the wheelchair, closed and locked the backdoor of the van, stepped over to the passenger door, opened it, collected my stuff from Rona's lap into the pockets of my pants and settled her into the wheelchair. Two minutes later we closed a pretty dramatic night in the safety of our room at the exclusive   hotel.

52

About six in the next morning Rona woke me up saying isn't it time to leave, Michael? I yawned sure Rona. Let's go down to the fine restaurant below, consume that huge breakfast they serve, and then I'll be ready to fly you and that old relic back to Israel in no time. Piece of cake.

Forty minutes later we left the restaurant on our way back to the elevator. I said just a minute, Rona, and walked over to the hotel's cashier desk. Asked in my best French if I owe them something. The young woman sitting behind the desk replied in French no, Mr. Legrand, everything has been taken care of. Thirty minutes after that we were seated in the white van, our luggage in the back, and departed. Where now, Michael? inquired Rona. To the central train station, of course, baby. She smiled widely and approved, by all means, Michael. We've been there just yesterday, but it seems ages ago.

Another twenty minutes' drive through the center of town, and I parked the van in a large subterranean garage below the Gare Cornavin. I said sorry, Rona, you better stay here in watch duty over the precious box while I go up to the station area above, ten-fifteen minutes max. She said sure, Michael. But please remove the lid and put the relic next to me so I can have a look at it's content while you're away, as hard as it may be to examine it inside the crate.

I took an elevator from the parking area to the ground floor and from there to a large hall with many public phone booths. Stepped inside one of those, called Kaplan on his cell phone and spoke five minutes with him. Then spotted another office in the station area, next to the Geneva   tourism booth. Walked over to the glass sliding door of that particular office,   marked TPG. It slid wide open automatically before me and I stepped in, wore my best seducer's grin at the blonde middle aged woman making her best to look busy by a desk featuring a small laminating machine, walked over to the counter facing her, took out one passport picture of myself and another of Rona and announced nonchalantly,

"I'll buy two 'Cartes Oranges' please."

The blonde woman came to the business side of the counter, smiled in my face and demanded,

"Identity cards, please."

I gave her our fake Swiss IDs. She examined them and said,

"Very well, Mr. Legrand. That will be 140 Francs, for two monthly passes valid for unlimited use of the Geneva tram/bus system. It will take about ten minutes. Why don't you have a seat."

She turned back to the desk while I sat patiently on a red couch next to the sliding door. It took her actually somewhat less then ten minutes to hand me two orange colored laminated cards bearing the names of Mr. and Mrs. Legrand below my photo and Rona's, respectively. I said merci beaucoup, took the cards and returned to the van in the parking lot. Rona glared a real hot welcome at me, and stated,

"This ossuary is very, very exciting. Michael. We must get it back to Jerusalem, cost what may."

I replaced the lid over the precious object, then recovered it with the long black coat and removed it to the back of the van, proclaiming,

"Sure. Rona. We'll get it to Ben Gurion airport before nightfall today."

On that note I started the engine and drove the white van into the slow morning rush hour traffic of a midweek working day, following the road signs indicating Geneva International Airport, Cointrin. It was going to take us almost an hour to get there in this kind of traffic. But that was Okay. Just enough time for Kaplan to fly his Astra SPX corporate jet from Klotten airport in Zurich and land it in Cointrin.

"What's the plan now, Rambo," laughed Rona. "Are you going to storm the airport with you pistol, kill any and all armed men of the opposition, take the girl and the treasure, and fly happily off into the sky?"

"You've got the last part, but not the beginning. We don't need to shoot here. This is Switzerland, not the Middle East, remember? The last time they fought a war here was back in the Renaissance. They don't have our security conscious mindset. They also generally think in a different way. Straight, by the book. Linear reasoning, point A to point B. Not like in Israel, where daily life revolves around improvisations and circular, hidden combinations. It's not a matter of different intelligence but of a completely different mentality.

We'd just use some chutzpa, a term Swiss people wouldn't even be able to fully understand, and we'd get ourselves with Boney in the Box smack into Kaplan's bizjet."

"Great. Can you be a little more specific on the details of this genial plan that you've devised, my man?"

"It's not my solo idea this time around, honey. I improvised it just now over the telephone with Kaplan. Here, take this orange colored card bearing your photo. It's a monthly pass for use of the Geneva tram and bus public transportation system. But it looks almost identical to the temporary identification badges issued to airport employees in Cointrin. Most companies servicing the airport use white vans, similar to ours. There are two service entrances to the tarmac. One called Pres-Bois and the other C5. We'll go to C5, which is a service entrance allowing access to the airplanes for small cars and vans, including catering vans, show these orange cards to the guard at the gate, and hope she or he is a regular Swiss person. Don't ask me what my back up plan is, cause I haven't thought about it yet."

53

We came near the Cointrin airport complex at about 9:50 in the morning. It was constructed on a southwest to northeast axis, with the main terminal slightly off center to the north. I drove the van past a "Sky Guide" panel, then to the right of it between two large parking lots and then turned left next to the south wall of the main terminal. There was a small entrance way to the tarmac there. It indicated C5. I drove the white van into that road. The entrance was blocked by an electrically operated gate. I drove forward and stopped short of the gate. Rona smiled to the security guard seated in a booth to its right side and showed him her orange identity card. He came out of the booth over to my side of the van, still standing several meters away from me. I showed him my orange card. He nodded, returned to the booth, the gate opened and we drove the white van inside the airport area. A roadway on our right led into the cargo area and the general aviation apron site just behind it. I drove the van to the right about fifty meters to the tie down general aviation apron lot. Two executive twin engine Learjets were parked there. No Astra SPX.

I drove the van out of the general aviation parking lot, on an asphalt road next to a taxiway past a few small general aviation hangars, stopped it short of the taxiway, cut the engine and stepped out. Shaded my eyes and gazed to the gliding approach to runway 23. No Astra SPX. Then I examined the airplanes circling the traffic pattern around the runway and saw it just turning base above my head. I recognized the Astra by the low swept wings with winglets, twin rear fuselage mounted engines, abnormally sharp looking nose, swept tail fin and low mounted stabilizer. The fuselage was painted in black over grey stripes from nose to tail. I conjectured that Kaplan probably had this toy of his fashion designed at Pierre Cardin's.

A few minutes later the Astra landed, taxied toward us, passed by us and stopped at the general aviation apron lot. The engines' roar gradually subsided, the left door opened and a spotless staircase extended electrically to the asphalt. The very tall figure of Bruce Kaplan, dressed up with a striped black and grey latest fashion suite, waived splendidly at us and made a magnificent descent. He then went over to the passenger door of the van, where Rona had already lowered the window and extended her right arm to him. He kissed her hand and offered gallantly,

"Shall I carry you aboard, Rona?"

I made "No, buddy. I'll carry her aboard, and you can open the cargo hold and put this wooden crate and our luggage in there. Secure it well and I'll return to take Rona's wheelchair."

He complied and pulled the crate out, still covered with my long black overcoat. Put his finger through the bullet hole into the right pocket of the coat and sighed,

"Always sloppy, Michael. I could never figure out what on earth women find in you. I hope you'll throw this crumpled thing in the garbage and get yourself something decent. Maybe I'd come over to Israel and force you to enter some Tel Aviv boutiques with me to buy real clothes for you."

I carried Rona up the staircase into the plane and turned right to settle her comfortably into one of the elegant leather armchairs in the passenger cabin. But she said no Michael, put me in the cockpit on the right side pilot's seat. I said yeah, sure, I could use a good co-pilot. So I secured her in that seat and returned to the van below, hugged Kaplan and said thanks pal, your country owes you a zillion. He bent down, kissed me on the cheek and blurted,

"Take the wheelchair and fly out of here, monkey face."

54

The sky was covered with heavy black clouds and large raindrops were collecting on the windshield of the SPX when I was cleared for take- off on runway 23. Pushed the throttle all the way in, reached take- off wind speed about thirty seconds after that, pulled the stick up and ascended into the stormy sky at 3805 feet per minute. Lightning struck the ground below us just as we entered the clouds. I climbed over the clouds flying by the instruments, above the cumulonimbus ceiling into the bright late morning sunlight. When the altimeter indicated thirty- one thousand feet I reduced rpm, leveled the stick to the long range cruising speed of 800 km/h and took the VOR direction over the Mont Blanc, as instructed by air traffic control at Cointrin. As we passed over the Massif I indicated below saying,

"See, baby. If I hadn't managed to grab the railing for dear life at the Aiguille du Midi down there when Kalman catapulted me over last week I'd still not have reached the valley floor. "

"Lucky for me, Michael. And for him," she motioned to the cargo hold behind and below us.

"What about him, indeed. Learned anything new? You did have some time to look at the bone box earlier."

"I did have a look. I wish I could examine it more carefully, but what I saw was mesmerizing enough."

"Okay, Rona. You're just dying to tell me. So why don't you start with the inscription just to the left of the Taw or Chi mark, that large sideways tilted cross I already saw back at Frankenheim's dungeon."

"On the narrow side, just under the rim of the ossuary, preceded by that mark, there's an inscription consisting of eleven letters in the same square Hebrew script we use today in Israel."

"I've seen that, Rona. But I couldn't read it properly back at the chateau with Frankenheim pointing a gun at me. The leftmost letters are clearer, right? They say something like 'abaryehosef'?"

"Bar Yehoself is Aramaic for 'son of Joesph.' The 'a' you could make out preceding the patronym is the last letter of four in the first name."

"What's the first name, then?"

The incisions of the first three letters are more difficult to read. But I believe they are Yod-Shin-Vav. The only letter which is different from our Hebrew script of today is the second letter-Shin. That's because it's written in a somewhat different form, with two teeth of the fork pointing to the right, instead of three teeth pointing upward. But that particular peculiarity probably appears also on other inscriptions from the first century. These three letters together with the fourth letter, which is Ayn, make for 'Yeshua'."

"You mean like 'Salvation' in Hebrew? That's a strange name."

"It does sound exactly like the Hebrew word for 'salvation,' except that the proper spelling of that would be 'Yeshuah.' But the Heh is silent in Hebrew just like an H in English. The only difference in sound could be that the accent would be on the last syllable in 'Yeshuah' and on the second syllable in 'Yeshua.' So you're basically correct. 'Yeshua' stands for 'salvation.' It's a contraction of the much more common Hebrew name 'Yehoshua' which means 'God will save.' 'Yeshua' is a rather unusual name, occurring only twice in the Old Testament, never in the Mishna and only by way of interpretation in the Talmud."

"The spelling of the father's name is also strange, Rona. Isn't Joseph always spelled Yod-Vav-Samekc-Peh, 'Yosef'? Never heard of a spelling with the additional Heh like on this bone box, 'Yehosef'."

"It appears in this spelling, 'Yehosef', indeed only once in the Old Testament. And there's no such spelling at all in post biblical ancient Jewish writings, such as the Mishna from the second century and the Talmud. On the other hand the regular spelling, 'Yosef' without the Heh, is very common. Scores, maybe hundreds of occurrences in the Old Testament, the Mishna, the Talmud and other ancient Hebrew writings."

"So they transferred the Heh from the son's name to the father's? Maybe there's some symbolic significance to that. The letter Heh stands for God in Jewish tradition, because it's part of his actual, holy name."

"Right you are. The very contraction of the ineffable name of God. The Tetragrammaton."

"So the contraction of 'Yehoshua' to 'Yeshua' and the concurrent, parallel extension of 'Yosef' into 'Yehosef' is meant to convey a deeper meaning, that Yeshua bar Yehosef is not the God of the Old Testament himself, but rather the son of Joseph and of that other God, our own God of the Old Testament, concurrently?"

"Maybe there is symbolism in it, and maybe there isn't. I believe the form of spelling of at least 'Yehosef' was actually found on other ossuaries from the first century. They also found some ossuaries with the contraction 'Yeshua,' which may just be commemorative. But your supposition appears well founded, Michael, as the symbolism you suggest seems to conform precisely with one of the main doctrines of Christianity. The dual nature of Jesus of Nazareth. I for one never believed much in coincidences."

"So this bone box indicates Jesus?"

"That's what the name 'Yeshua bar Yehosef' literally is when transcribed into English, Michael."

Jesus, son of Joseph.

55

It was Instrument Flight Rules on approach to Ben Gurion Airport, with low storm   clouds covering the coastal plain, Tel Aviv and Jerusalem. I followed the ILS signal through the clouds and landed smoothly onto runway 12. Taxied the   Astra to the general aviation area, cut the engines off, parked and secured the plane. A blue van marked Israel Antiquities Authorities stopped next to the Astra. Zalman Ganot came out and shook my hand. I transferred to him possession of the wooden box containing the ossuary. He expressed,

"Thank you Inspector, you've achieved a great thing bringing this one back."

"You don't know what that required, Ganot. I hope it's the real thing, at least."

"It is."

"What makes you so sure, Zalman?"

"In my bones, Inspector. In my bones."

"What about the rest of the ossuaries it was found with?"

"We have them all in a safe place."

"But aren't you finally going to tell me more about them?"

"I told you once my hands are tied on this, Michael. Can't tell you more than I did."

"I understand that, pal. All in the line of duty."

"Exactly. We're all serving the same country, Inspector."

'Isn't the Antiquities Authority ever going to expand about the finds made in Dov Gruner street in 1980? You can't keep this a secret from all the people, all the time."

He shook my hand,

"Well thanks again to you, Inbar. You deserve a medal but I doubt you'd ever get one. An article about the 1980 East Talpiot find has just been released in our Authority's periodical publication, called 'Atiqot'. Read volume 29, pages 15-22, entitled 'A tomb with inscribed ossuaries in East Talpiot,' if you can find the volume. Take care."

Rona and I returned to live in her apartment and to our police positions, nine to five. I practically discarded this affair from my mind when one day Leora called inquiring about my mental well- being. I said it's somewhat better now. Still very depressed but hanging on. Of course I will never recover since I can't get Guy back into my daily life. But I continue holding him in my heart, and as long as I live he'll have a presence in this world. Leora asked what about that investigation , it seemed to invigorate you a bit. That thing with the ancient death relics. I told her about the 'Atiqot' article that Zalman Ganot suggested. She said I'll get it for you. Do your utmost to stay on life's surface in the meantime, Michael. I promise I'll get you that article.

Two weeks later Leora called again, said listen to this Michael. It's about that article. Turns out it's next to impossible to lay hands on it. Can you tell me why that is,? I said no. Not now. What happened exactly, Leora? She detailed,

"I first went to the Tel Aviv University library. Found the 'Atiqot' publication, but only through 1974. Went to the Bar Ilan library, same negative result. They had the publication readily available but not volume 29. They said someone must have checked it out. The librarian there suggested it may be found in other countries. Best try in the United States. I called an old friend of mine, Paula Libling, who lives in Los Angeles. She said sure, I'd try to get you this article. Yesterday I got an email from her on this subject. I just forwarded it to you. Read that and let's discuss this peculiar matter after you're done. Bye. The children miss you, come to visit them soon. I love you too."

I got the forwarded email to her from Paula Libling, and read a diary style account of a chase for an elusive article:

"Hi Leora. As to that article you wanted, I did a lot to get it, and couldn't thus far. I first went to the University of Judaism, just across the hill from my house, in Bel Aire. They have a pretty substantial library. I looked through it and found several early volumes of the periodical published by the Israel Antiquities Authority, but they didn't have anything recent. The girl who was on duty as librarian said to come another day when the head librarian is in. He's pretty good, she said. So I came again two days later and spoke to that middle aged man. He seemed very professional, told me after a few minutes the University of Judaism does not have the volume I wanted, 'Atiqot' number 29. But he also did a thorough check for me in other libraries. Then he handed me an address of a theological seminar in Pasadena, called 'Fuller'. The next morning I drove over there. It's a nice quiet campus, with an impressive four story building dedicated to the library. The librarian checked on her computer, said yes we do have 'Atiqot,' on the second floor. I went there and found the entire series, nice volumes bound in red hardcover. But volume 29 was missing. It was the only volume missing. I searched the work desks in the reading area, zilch. So I returned down to the librarian. She checked again in her documents and on her computer and informed that they got the entire series from the publisher, except for volume 29. They wrote the publisher several times and never got a response. Sorry. But she checked further and said Berkeley University has the 'Atiqot' series. I called a friend who studies on campus in Berkeley. A day later he called back and what do you think? Berkeley has the entire series, with the notable exception of volume 29. What in the world does this mean?"

I scratched my head, emailed Leora, cc: Paula Libling "Just forget it, girls. I appreciate your efforts, but this apparently depends on a higher power." Then I took Rona out to dinner at the Neve Sha'ananim restaurant, in panoramic view of the Old City walls and the Tower of David. It was a French-Moroccan style restaurant, similar in culinary art to the Casbah restaurant in Tel Aviv where our romance took off on its hottest note, when she was my own woman in red.

56

I guess the ossuaries affair would have remained buried for me after I'd reached that dead end, if fate had not decided otherwise.

On March 4, 1996, the eve of the Purim holiday, I took Rona down to Tel Aviv. We strolled through the vibrant city, so different in temperament from our own Jerusalem, enjoying a very good time. Then around 2:45 P.M. we decided to go shopping in the newest mall of Tel Aviv, called Dizengoff Center. We cleared a good amount of money from our joint account, then exited to fashionable Dizengoff street, one of the main shopping neighborhoods in Tel Aviv, aligned with avant-garde art stores and boutiques. We were standing on the curb next to the bus station. I looked at my watch. It was 4:09 P.M. I proposed,

"Hey Rona. Why don't we go visit your friend Yael, over at her charming one storey house on Chen boulevard. That's about a ten minutes walk from here."

She nodded happily in consent, and I started pushing her wheelchair eastbound, toward King George street. At that point a young man wearing a heavy overcoat brushed me, hurrying to the bus behind us. He was just about Guy's age and I turned my head back to look at him boarding the steps of the bus, as I did many times, watching live young men about that age and ruminating how Guy also could have been enjoying youthful existence. Why did he have to commit suicide? Then lightning struck my brain in realization that the Arab looking young man boarding the bus was also going to commit suicide. But as opposed to Guy who did that in the privacy of his own bedroom, this one was going to kill as many other people as he possibly could, just for being Jews. I leaped over Rona and covered her with my body, just when a blast of incredible heat scorched my back and all hell broke loose around us.

When I lifted my head I saw Rona wasn't injured, and took a first look at the scene of total panic.

The entire Dizengoff center looked like a battleground. About ten cars were blown apart in the street. Fire Department trucks were blasting sirens. Police then came and started clearing unhurt people from the area for fear of a second explosive device. I saw some mutilated bodies lying about the demolished bus. Then paramedics came and transported me to the Ichilov hospital. Rona demanded they take her along to watch me and so they did. I was checked at the hospital's emergency room and transported to an intensive care unit, Rona seated on her wheelchair next to my bed. We heard the nurses saying two other victims of the attack in very critical condition were also brought to Ichilov and just died of their wounds. Three victims were in emergency surgery. Five including myself were in various intensive care units and three were awaiting surgery. During the next two days doctors examined me thoroughly and I was given many tests. After that they said I could be released, but stay out of work for at least six weeks. On the TV they reported over 130 persons were treated in six different hospitals. Thirteen people have been killed. In the Peres government emergency meeting the establishment of a new unit was agreed upon, to deal specifically with suicide terrorism. Because the latest attack came after a suicide bombing on another bus about ten days before and two other suicide bombing attacks in between.

Rona said I was so worried for you Michael. Let's go to vacation for the next six weeks, since you can't go to work. I said fine. On the next day we boarded a flight to London, England. Little did we know that of all places the ossuaries affair was going to reopen for us there.

57

If I were religious I would probably have believed that a sign from heaven occurred on the first clear skied Sunday of our stay in London, just when we were sharing a small space of Hyde Park garden with many milk skinned locals, for whom a sunny day was something that called for stripping naked and soaking the rays in. That scene looked really bizzare to us. In our native Israel the majority of post puberscents most of the time seek the shade rather than searing ultraviolet solar emissions.

From out of the soft light a very, very tall blonde woman, about Rona's age, strode toward us exclaiming in a heavy Scandinavian accent,

"Hi Mickey, do you remember me?"

"Sure thing," I grinned. "Rona, meet Marit Olson. Marit this is Rona Argov."

Rona eyed me with a bemused expression, rating,

"Not bad. What did you do with her, Michael. Climb a chair?"

"That's a good one," laughed Marit. "I would have loved to, he could use a ladder. But he was solidly married at the time I came across. Or rather he came across. He was strictly on duty, saved me from some bad guys in East Jerusalem who thought they could rape me. Sensing the magnetic field connecting the haloes around you beautiful couple, I guess he's taken again. So I'll leave you. I just came to spend a weekend from Oxford, where I'm doing a Ph.D in theology. Here's my card. If you visit that university town you're invited for Swedish coffee and smorgasbord. Take care."

Exactly two weeks later we used the card, called her and made an appointment at her Oxford apartment for the next day. Here's why.

We were strolling down Oxford street. We came before a   newspaper stand and Rona requested,

"Please buy me a newspaper, Michael. My curiosity hasn't had news of the world for too many days. Get the London Sunday Times."

I complied and brought that to her. She went over the headlines, then stopped cold and indicated the front page, saying look Michael, look at this!

It was a long article under a bold headline, proclaiming

"The Tomb that Dare Not Speak its Name."

58

"This story in the March 31, 1996 London Times reports that in addition to the ossuary inscribed with the name 'Jesus, son of Joseph' five other ossuaries inscribed with names were found in the East Talpiot tomb," said Rona. "Here they are:

2. 'Joseph;'
3. 'Mary;'
4. 'Mary;'
5 'Matthew;'
6. 'Juda, son of Jesus.'

The story infers that the second Mary is Mary Magdalen. It also announces that the ossuaries were empty when they were found. That the bones of Joseph, Mary, Jesus son of Joseph, the other Mary and the rest of the family had already been vandalized, probably in antiquity."

"Why would anybody want to take old bones from a family grave," I said. "That simply doesn't make sense. I wish we had that article we were looking for, to see if it says anything about the bones in the ossuaries."

"I have the article and I'll bring it," said Marit. "I searched and found it after you called about this London Times story. In general I'd say that the intactness of bones was very important to early Christians, notably when the bones belonged to Jesus. Thus the author of the Fourth Gospel warns that 'not one of his bones will be broken.' Similarly the apostle Paul writes in his epistle to the Ephesians, 5:30, 'we are all members of his body and of his bones.' But before I go into that, let me tell you three things. First, Jesus had a sister named Mary. So the second Mary could be that sister. Second, Jesus had a brother named Joseph, nicknamed 'Joses', so the 'Joseph' could be that brother or his father. Third, Jesus also had a first cousin named Matthew. He was a customs agent, son of Joseph's brother Alphaeus/Clopas. So all these names actually conform exactly with Jesus' family as per the New Testament."

"But in that case who is 'Judah son of Jesus'?" I queried. "If Jesus had a son, then the second Mary must logically have been not his sister, but his wife. Would she then have been Mary Magdalene?"

"Possibly, but not necessarily" said Marit. "Jesus also had very intimate contact with another Mary, sister of Martha from Bethany, who has anointed his feet and dried them with her hair, per John 12:3. In another passage of John, Jesus is said specifically to have loved these same sisters."

"I remember the ossuary that I recovered first is inscribed in Greek with both the names Mary and Martha. Maybe that's how she or they got their ticket to the Talpiot tomb."

Rona said "If that ossuary contained the bones of two women, they must have been sisters, because burial together of two unrelated women was forbidden under Jewish Law."

I queried "But how could Jesus' family afford a rock hewn tomb? I thought they were a poor family."

Marit replied "Jesus' family was of Davidic descent. You know that's absolutely the most exalted birth in Judaism. They couldn't possibly be of the lowest social class, that couldn't afford a decent tomb. The historian Josephus in his work 'Antiquity of the Jews' actually describes Jesus' brother James as a very prominent person. In any event, Jesus had some fabulously rich supporters like Joseph of Arimatea and Nicodemus, who could fund the Talpiot tomb for his family."

Marit went to her studio and returned with a volume marked "Atiqot 29." She leafed through it and informed,

"Here's what this says. It reports specifically that 'the bones within these ossuaries were in an advanced stage of disintegration.' Now why would the London Times' reporters   have been told there were no bones found in the ossuaries when the family tomb was unearthed in 1980, if the ossuaries actually did contain the bones at that time?"

"Weren't Jesus' hands nailed to the cross?" said I. "Maybe they found forensic evidence of precisely such nailing of the hand or palm bones in the ossuary inscribed 'Jesus, son of Joseph' and they don't want anybody to know that?"

Marit nodded her head and commented, "Another interesting find   the Sunday Times article mentions is 'a broken mark supposedly of a fish.' The mark of the fish was an early symbol of the Jesus sect, being a figurative expression of a famous Christian acrostic in Greek , meaning ' Jesus Christ, God's son, Savior,' the initial letters of which spell the Greek word for 'fish'."

"But if you read the Sunday Times' article carefully, it isn't clear whether this fish drawing was part of the finds in the Jesus family tomb," commented Rona. "It talks about a 'second Jesus ossuary' two sentences prior to mentioning the fish drawing."

"The article specifically talks about a 'Six inch diameter piece of pottery' in logical continuation of the report about the fish mark." Marit responded. "Coupled with the Atiqot article, which specifies that a few shards were found in the tomb, I'd say the fish mark was most probably drawn on a pottery shard found in the subject tomb. I'm pretty certain that the reporter simply confused 'ossuary' with 'ostracon,' which is an inscribed pottery shard. But I guess one would have to ask the reporter to redraft more precisely on that point, to be absolutely certain."

"But if the fish symbolizes that Christian acrostic in Greek talking about the divine Christ, how could it be used in Judea, Marit?" I asked.

"Good point for polemics, Michael. As Jesus himself said on one famous occasion when people in Nazareth expressed their disinterest in him, 'No prophet is respected at home.' But the fact is that the fish was already a symbol of the Jesus sect in first century Judea."

I wondered, "Jesus is the origin of the saying 'no prophet is acceptable in his town'? I thought this was a Jewish proverb, Marit."

"It was," said Rona. "Thus in the Old Testament the shepherd-prophet Amos was unwelcome in Bethel because he was a Judean; 'Go home and prophesy there' he was told by the high priest of Samaria. Similarly according to the Dead Sea Scrolls a prophet should be treated as a teacher of falsehood by members of a different tribe while hailed as a herald of truth by members of his own clan."

"Maybe that's why Jesus wasn't buried in Nazareth," I opined.

"Interesting," said Marit. "I haven't thought of this. The fact is that also here in England dissidents used to be buried apart from regular folks. We have a cemetery in London demonstrating that."

"Which cemetery is that? I'd like to visit it," said Rona.

"It's called Bunhill Field. Aptly enough, this name is most probably a corruption of 'Bonehill'."

59

On the next morning we went to Bunhill Fields, in the heart of the City of London, where Rona informed,

"I've read some on this cemetery yesterday, Michael. It was used for the burial of nonconformists in the 18th century, but is now as you can see a public park. It was operated as a burial ground for 'dissenters' from 1665 to 1853, during which time around 123,000 burials took place. There are many notable graves, including John Bunyan, William Blake, Daniel Defoe, many of the Cromwell family and Susanna Wesley, mother of the founder of Methodism."

"Very nice, Rona. Reverting to Jesus and his family tomb, is that the reason that it wasn't located in Nazareth?"

"Could be. But the location in East Talpiot is very close to Bethlehem, actually about midway on the old road between Bethlehem and Jerusalem. In the first century, because of purity concerns, burials were never made inside towns and villages. Come to think of it, East Talpiot is just the place you'd expect Jeusalemites, and, even more so, people from Bethlehem, to be buried. So it was logical for Jesus' family to have a burial cave in East Talpiot."

"But wasn't Jesus' family from Nazareth, Rona?"

"His immediate family lived in Nazareth during his childhood. But the family originated from Bethlehem. This is specifically stated in the New

Testament. Thus Luke accounts that Joseph and Mary had to go to Bethlehem when the Romans carried out a census in the holy land, because 'all went to their own towns to be registered. Joseph also went from the town of Nazareth in Galilee to Judea, to the city of David called Bethlehem, because he was descended from the house and family of David. He went to be registered with Mary, to whom he was engaged and who was expecting a child. While they were there, the time came for her to deliver her child'."

"That's interesting. If Joseph and the pregnant Mary couldn't take the census in Nazareth but had to take it in Bethlehem, that would probably indicate that they actually had a legal connection to Bethlehem, not to Nazareth."

"Right, Michael. Come to think of it, this requirement would establish that Bethlehem was their Domicilium under Roman law. That basically means that they had no intention to reside in Nazareth permanently. Therefore it would have made little sense for them to have a family tomb in Nazareth, that they wouldn't be able to frequently visit at a later stage in their lives. They would have wanted a family tomb close to Bethlehem and Jerusalem, easily accessible also to future generations of the family."

"But in that case, why was Jesus called 'of Nazareth'?"

"The traditional name of Jesus in Hebrew, as reflected also in the Talmud, is 'Yeshu Hanotzri'. This appellation stems from 'Netzer'- shoot or branch. It alludes to Isaiah 11:1, indicating the Royal birth of

Jesus, to substantiate his claim for Jewish messiahship. Not to indicate the place he comes from."

We continued walking in the park in silence, then came to a tomb in a fairly central position between the City Road and Bunhill Row, across the road from Wesley's chapel. Rona read,

"Thomas Bayes, born 1702, died 1761. Do you know who he was, Michael?"

"I'm not sure. The statistician?"

"Right Michael. He was a mathematician who first used probability inductively and established a mathematical basis for probability inference. He set down his findings on probability in an essay published after his death."

"I wonder what he would have said about the probability of the East Talpiot family tomb being the real thing."

"I'm sure he would have said it's a slam dunk, or some similar expression in 18th century lingo."

"But the names on the East Talpiot ossuaries were probably very common in first century Judea, Rona. How would that play out?"

"I knew that Thomas Bayes was buried here, Michael and I've done some homework on this very intriguing subject. In fact I've gotten the 'Tal Ham' list of Jewish names mentioned in the Sunday Times article, which is in fact 'Tal Ilan.' Here it is

She produced a book from her handbag, entitled Lexicon of Jewish Names in Late Antiquity, Part 1: Palestine 330 BCE - 200 CE and continued,

"The book contains the names of 3,595 people, of which 2,826 were statistically valid (the remaining names were doubtful).

Here are some general statistics concerning the population and valid names:

Population with valid male names: 2,509
Population with valid female names: 317
Total : 2,826

Male names: 721
Female names: 110
Total: 831

Most popular names:

Male	Female
1. Simon	Mariam
2. Joseph	Salome
3. Judah	Shelamzion
4. Eleazar	Martha
5. Yohanan	Joanna
6. Joshua	Shiphra
7. Hananiah	Berenice
8. Jonathan	Sarah
9. Menahem	Imma
10.Jacob	Mara

Names divided according to language (male and female):

Biblical: 166

Greek: 244
Latin: 84
Persian: 37
Semitic-Hebrew: 243
Semitic-Greek: 57

"What does all this boil down to, Rona?"

"I've emailed these numbers to a statistician friend who lives in Canada, and here's the detailed explanation I received from him:

'The following assumptions (except for the size of Jerusalem and the chance of Mary's name appearing) are very conservative:

1. Assume that the probability of the name "Mary" occurring in a family is 1 in 2.9 (two Marys);

2. Assume that the probability of the name "Joseph" occurring in a family is 1 in 6.3;

3. Assume that the probability of the name "Judah" occurring in a family is 1 in 6.6;

4. Assume that the probability of the name "Jesus" occurring in a family is 1 in 11.9;

5. Assume that the probability of the name "Matthew" occurring in a family is 1 in 14.9;

6. Assume that the population of Jerusalem at the time of Jesus was 25,000 (according to the scholar Jeremia) [Note some sources report a much larger population size, likely because of the larger number of people present during special days];

7. Assume that the average family size was 6 (likely much larger).

Also assume that the same name does not occur in a family more than once (except for "Mary" since one might have been part of the family by marriage). By eliminating each successive name from the total, the following is the revised reduced probabilities:

1. Assume that the probability of the name "Mary" occurring in a family is 1 in 2.9 (two Marys);

2. Assume that the probability of the name "Joseph" occurring in a family is 1 in 6.3;

3. Assume that the probability of the name "Judah" occurring in a family is 1 in 5.6;

4. Assume that the probability of the name "Jesus" occurring in a family is 1 in 8.2;

5. Assume that the probability of the name "Matthew" occurring in a family is 1 in 9.0;

6. Assume that the population of Jerusalem at the time of Jesus was 25,000 (according to the scholar Jeremia);

7. Assume that the average family size was 6 (likely much larger).

Thus, the probability of the six "common" names occurring in one family of the time is:

1/2.9 x 1/2.9 x 1/6.3 x 1/5.6 x 1/8.2 x 1/9.0 = 1/21,897

Approximate number of families = 25,000/6 = 4,167

Therefore, out of 21,897 families, this particular combination of common names might occur just once. However, in Jerusalem at the time, there were only about a fifth of this number of families. Thus the likelihood that this was Jesus' family is almost certain. Even if Jerusalem was five times the reported population size (i.e. 125,000), there would still be no more than one family with this particular combination of names'."

60

In the evening of the next Sunday, April 7, 1996 we were relaxing in our guestroom at a hotel in the city of Lincoln. We had previously visited the old part of this city, blessed with an abundance of fourteenth and fifteenth century buildings and a large number of half-timbered Tudor houses. We saw the oldest bridge in England to have houses built on it, the Lincoln Castle and the third largest Cathedral in Britain. All this made for a very exhausting day.

I opened the TV set and minutes later the BBC aired a special program for Easter. It was a documentary hosted by Joan Bakewell, CBE , entitled "The Body in Question." It basically restated the information given a week earlier in the Sunday Times article. One of the participants declared that "it felt like the balls of the National Lottery coming one by one," and another announced, "it is remarkable." The host of the broadcast vocalized ,"We stood dumbfounded by the sensational nature of what was before our eyes. The names of Jesus, Joseph and Mary are luminous with meaning for anyone brought up in the Christian tradition. Our finds will renew the debate of the Resurrection and deepen the mystery surrounding Easter."

Rona exclaimed, "I just realized that today is precisely 1966 years since Jesus' crucifixion. That happened on April 7, 30 A.D. Isn't that remarkable, Michael?"

I stepped out to the small balcony of our guestroom and took in the view of the historic city, rising majestically from the north banks of the river Witham, on a slope crowned by its beautiful triple-towered cathedral, overlooking miles of green countryside. I mused several minutes about closure of cycles in death and life, then returned to the room, kissed Rona with passion and declared I adore you, honey. Let's return to Jerusalem.

61

Seventeen months later the doorbell rang in our Jerusalem apartment. I went to open the door. It was the mailman, who gave me a brown paper bound package, addressed to 'Inbar, Yemin Moshe.' I opened the package and found a large album style book, entitled <u>A catalogue of Jewish Ossuaries in the Collections of the State of Israel.</u> By L. Rahmani. Upon opening the first page I found a business card of Zalman Ganot, scribbled, "Best wishes. Refer to numbers 701-709. See also number 140."

I swore between my teeth "I know these games of yours already too well, Zalman." Opened at number 701 of the catalogue, on page 222, and began reading.

It was a detailed, professional description of the ossuaries found in the East Talpiot family tomb.

Item number 701 was the ossuary of which I'd examined a Polaroid photo taken almost two years before at Kibbutz Sde Eliahu, the one inscribed in Greek "Mariamene who is Mara." In the commentary below the description of the name, the author stated "The department (of Antiquities) retained nine ossuaries (nos. 701-709) recovered from a double-chambered loculi and arcoolia tomb in 1980; a plain, broken specimen was also found." Then the author deemed important to add the following unusual acknowledgment: "Thanks are due to the late J.Gath, the excavator, for granting permission to publish these ossuaries." The author commented on item 701 that the name Mariamene is one of the variants of the Hebrew name Miriam (Mary). The other name mentioned as a double name was Mara, a contraction of Martha;

Item number 702 was inscribed in Aramaic, with Hebrew script "Yehuda bar Yeshua."- Judah, son of Jesus;

Item number 703 was inscribed in Hebrew "Matya." The commentary said this is a contraction of "Matityahu."-Matthew.

Item number 704 carried a symbol on the lid, narrow side, which looked like a six pointed star. Essentially the combination of a cross mark and a vertical stroke. By that time Rona had already showed me the archeology book I first saw at Moshe Cohen's apartment, which explained that a monogram like this was actually composed of the initial Greek letters of the name Jesus and the title Christ, i.e. Iota and Chi, written together. That book said such monogram could therefore be an abbreviation, in a ligature, of the name and title, Jesus Christ; and that the Chi could also be considered the mark of the Cross, and the vertical mark as the initial and abbreviation of the name of Jesus.

On the narrow side , under the rim, stood the large Taw mark, the Cross or the Chi, sign of the Messiah, preceding the name Jesus, son of Joseph, that I'd already known from before;

Item number 705 on the upper half, left of center, bore the inscription in Hebrew "Yose." The commentary said this is the equivalent of "Yosi," a contraction of "Yehosef"-Joseph. It continued to propose that the similarity of this ossuary and its inscription with that of Marya on item 706, both from the same tomb, may indicate that these are the ossuaries of the parents of Yeshua-Jesus (no. 704) and the grandparents of Yehuda-Judah (no. 702;)

Item number 706 on the upper half, center, bore the inscription in Hebrew "Marya."

The catalogue mentioned no names for items numbers 707 through 709.

Number 140 featured a pottery shard bearing an inscription "Yeshua" in Hebrew script inside a drawing of a fish. The catalogue stated " provenance unknown." But I recalled the mentioning of just such an artifact in the Sunday Times article about the Talpiot tomb.

I closed the catalogue, went over to one of the floor- to- ceiling high bookshelves flanking the living room, and placed it indistinctively among similar volumes there. Then I exited to the terrace and took in the panoramic view of Sultan's pool, a dry pool expanse, popular venue for open-air symphonies, rock concerts and similar events. Looked beyond the pool at Mt. Zion and the Benedictine contours of the Dormition Abbey, built on the site where Mary is said to have drifted off to eternal sleep, and at the Cenacle, the room washed in rays of the Jerusalem sunlight, considered traditionally the very room of the Last Supper, located beyond the Dormition Abbey above David's Tomb.

Rona was standing on the apartment's balcony, her erect figure framed by the windmill rising above our Jerusalem quarter of Yemin Moshe. She walked over to me in perfect gait and asked,

"What was it, Michael?"

I hugged her body standing close to me, almost at my height, and said,

"The mailman brought us some present from Zalman Ganot. "

"What was the present about, darling?"

"Nothing, Rona. Nothing much. I just placed it inside your bookshelf."

She pierced my eyes with that intense gaze of hers and submitted poignantly,

"Okay Michael. Paraphrasing an ancient wise man, I'd say- let the dead bury their ghosts."

I turned around and grabbed the stroller where our ten months old son was sitting, his green eyes mirroring me, his blond curls reflecting the blinding summer sunrays. I indicated the alleyway overgrown with bougainvillea, below the white shaded apartments of our enclave and offered,

"Let's take this toddler to promenade here. And let everything else go, honey. Just let it all go."

Encino, February 12, 2006

AUTHOR'S NOTE

I first learned about the East Talpiot family tomb in 1998, while doing research for a prior novel I wrote about early Christianity. At that time I read the text of the newspaper article that was published on March 31st, 1996 in the London Sunday Times, entitled "The Tomb that Dare Not Speak its Name," and also some comments about a BBC program that followed it on April 7th, 1996. I realized then the magnitude of the find but also the reasons that it wasn't given much publicity. I discussed this matter since with many of my friends. One of my close friends even suggested to go to Israel, buy the condominium built over the cave and open a private museum featuring the ossuaries there.

In the summer of 2005 I raised this matter in an Internet forum on early Christianity and Judaism called "Shilonites" where I regularly post. Most of the participants were interested and contributed posts on the subject, some enthusiastically and others skeptically. One of the participants posted a statistical evaluation of the find, based on statistical findings in a work on Jewish names in antiquity by Tal Ilan. I included this statistical evaluation verbatim in this novel. Another participant indicated the Finegan work in reference below for an illuminating study of Christian symbolism. I've learned from other participants a few other things that helped me formulate two paragraphs in the book. I want to thank them all.

In writing this novel I used mostly my own knowledge of source material and of Hebrew. Other than that I used the following works, exclusively:

1. Finegan, Jack, The Archeology of the New Testament. Princeton University Press, 1978;

2. Rahmany, L.Y. A Catalogue of Jewish Ossuaries in the collections of the State of Israel. Israel Antiquities Authority, Jerusalem 1994;

3. Kloner, A "A Tomb with Inscribed Ossuaries in East Talpiot, Jerusalem." Atiqot vol. 29, (1996) pp. 15-22.

Itamar Bernstein, February 2006.

426462

Made in the USA